DEAF HEAVEN

A NOVEL

CURTIS SMITH

RUNNING WILD

Paperback ISBN: 978-1-960018-78-6
eBook ISBN: 978-1-960018-77-9

Farewell, happy fields,
Where joy forever dwells! Hail, horrors! Hail,
Infernal World! and thou, profoundest Hell,
Receive thy new possessor—one who brings
A mind not to be changed by place or time.
The mind is its own place, and in itself
Can make a Heaven of Hell, a Hell of Heaven.

John Milton *Paradise Lost*

For the brokenhearted—and the hope of tomorrow

I

* * *

Two. Jason had now held two as they died. He squeezed the steering wheel. A grounding. A discharge of bad electricity. A man and a teenage girl, so different, yet when Jason pulled back, each considered him with open eyes, open mouths. Seeing, gasping—then not. Then the stillness. Then the warmth's fade. Then their slip into the pale sea, and in Jason, a different pull, an undertow that called from beyond the stars. He closed his eyes and saw not the darkness but a child on a sunbaked beach. A girl no taller than his waist. Her back to him and her feet in the surf. Her gaze lost upon the wide ocean.

He stepped from his car. The rowhomes and breezeways blurred by mist. Along the curb, ripped trash bags, the spill of wrappers and tin cans. This cold that stank of rotten meat. He thought of cop shows, the grainy images of surveillance cameras, and he pulled up his sweatshirt hood. A dog barked and another answered. A siren in the distance. Flannigan's neon shone red on the wet sidewalk. Jason hoisted a foot onto a stoop and pretended to tie his shoe. In high school, he'd acted in his senior play, urgings from his girlfriend and English teacher. The role, a lunkhead football star, hardly a stretch. Still Jason stammered and lost himself beneath the lights. The stakes higher now. His freedom. His life. He snuck the wallet and watch from his sweatshirt pocket, wiping each with his sleeve before setting them on the stoop.

A wince as he touched his forehead. The knot already rising. He stopped short of the bar entrance. The steam from his lips. The neon on his shoes. His childhood spent in this neighborhood. Then his escape to the suburbs while these streets crumbled. Crime. Drugs. Desperation. Another step,

3

the neon upon him. He'd grown up smelling booze in the bottom of a thousand left-behind glasses. He rarely drank, the curse in his blood, those years of uncertainty and violence. But tonight, he needed to collect himself. Tonight he needed a drink.

Inside, and for a bleary moment, the room's focus turned to him. A U-shaped bar, booths along one wall. A muted football game on the TV. The faces in the only occupied booth lifted from the dark as he passed. Beneath the TV, an old man. At the bar's other end, a pair of rough women. Their cigarettes shared an ashtray. Beauty parlor hair and lipstick on their glasses' rims. One scrolling through her phone. The other with a phlegmy cough. The bartender, silver-haired, thick in the gut and shoulders, took his order, and when Jason paid for his shot and beer with a crisp fifty, the women turned their dull gaze upon him.

On the jukebox, a country song, love gone wrong and a broken heart. Jason's hand trembled. A spill from his glass, his fingers wet. The burn in his throat. He touched the stain on his sweatshirt sleeve and wondered if it was blood. He lifted the glass and the bartender refilled it. In the liquid, the bar's warped lights. Around him, lazy rhythms and muffled voices. A strata of cigarette smoke. The bartop's damp rings and the rain carried on coats. By the door, a paper skeleton, hinged joints and a missing leg. Halloween last week, and ahead, winter's long white. Beside the door, a flier. **MISSING** in red letters, a little girl's smiling face. A photo he'd seen a hundred times. The story dominating the local news. Statements from the police and FBI. Her parents' tearful pleas. This ocean of sorrow.

He sipped his beer. He'd finish his drinks then fade back into the night. The alcohol calmed him, and he wove narratives for the others. Refugees. The ones too dim or too unlucky to outrun their shadows. He listened to the women's tipsy conversation and the sink's running water and the duct's push of tepid air. The sounds swirled, and the tide carried him to another dark room. An ultrasound's swoosh. A buried heartbeat. This ocean and all of them drowning.

The bartender worked a rag around a glass as he listened to the old man. Jason wouldn't have given them a second glance had it not been for the old man's repeated interjections of "Shitbird." *Shitbird*—it was the invective Jason's father had used when he was at his drunkest. The President was a shitbird. The mayor. The Phillies' manager. And most commonly, Jason was a shitbird.

Jason lifted his shot glass. The smell cut deep. His childhood. The man he swore he'd never be. Instead of throwing it back, he sipped half and let the bite linger. He closed his eyes and sank. An exhale through pursed lips, and with it, the memory of his daughter's pool summers. The twang of twin diving boards and their timed jumps, the released air at the well's bottom and their rise through a bubbled veil. Her smile waiting at the surface.

Jason's fifty now a clutch of smaller bills. The women to his right scrolled through their phones. "Shitbird," the old man piped, and the bartender nodded, perhaps in agreement, perhaps humoring him. The old man lit another cigarette, and his rheumy eyes disappeared between exhales. A lifetime had passed since Jason last saw his father. Physically, this man was in the ballpark—his age, his sun-splotched skin, his cigarette and yellow teeth—but more so, this place. These people. Shitbird. "Hey, shitbird."

Jason blinked. The old man was talking to him. "Hey, you, shitbird. What're you looking at?"

The old man ambled forward, his cigarette clenched between his lips. A bandy stride. Hunched shoulders. His fists clenched. Jason blinked again. This evening of bad dreams.

The bar's dazed attention upon him. His desire to quietly gather himself buried beneath the old man's shuffling steps. Jason had been a wrestler. High school trophies, college until he blew out his knee. He outweighed the old man by forty, maybe fifty pounds. Yet the sight of the old man, his sinew and menace, paralyzed Jason. A fear rooted in spine and gut.

The old man by his side. Jason glanced to the bartender, the women, wondering if they were seeing what he was. The bartender dried another glass. One of the women smiled from behind an exhaled cloud.

"Why're you staring at me?" The old man's voice of gravel and dust.

"I'm not—"

The old man stepped closer. His nose a roadmap of broken blood vessels. Twitches of smoke from the cigarette between his lips. "Don't tell me I can't believe my own goddamn eyes." With a flick, he knocked over Jason's beer. A cascade across the bartop. Jason's pants wet. His bills soaked. "There. Now you got no reason to stay."

One of the women blurted a stupid laugh. The old man blew smoke in Jason's face, and his voice reached through the haze. "Are you stupid? Are you a goddamn idiot? Why the fuck're you staring at me?"

Jason stood and wiped off his pants. He could only respond with the truth. "I thought maybe you were my father."

The old man turned to the bartender then to the ladies. All of them sharing his smile. In the next breath, the old man's expression crumpled, and he raised himself onto his tiptoes and smacked the back of Jason's head. The clank of his ring. His bony hand. "If I was your father, I would have knocked some goddamn sense into you long ago, you fucking shitbird."

The bartender laughed. One of the women held up her phone and snapped a picture. Jason turned, his wet bills left on the bar. The old man on his heels. A push against his back. "Fly, shitbird! Fly!"

The bar's laughter snuffed as the door closed behind him. A return to the night's cold drizzle. The dark street. The barking dogs. The stoop where he'd left the wallet and watch empty. He pulled up his hood and hurried to his car.

Home. This island. His body returned upon the flow. Alice rose from the couch. Her flannels and thick socks. An oversized sweatshirt, their college alma mater. Her blond ponytail and the broken nose from her field hockey days, the bump he liked to kiss, the assurance he loved her imperfections most of all. She asked her questions. *Where have you been? How did it go? Are you all right?* She stepped back, trying to read a truth he had yet to process. A flinch when she touched his forehead.

He brushed past her. Calm flames in the gas fireplace. Beyond, the dining room. The kitchen. The breakfast table. The patio's sliding doors. Alice had wanted an open floorplan, and Jason remembered his first time here. The realtor's repeated use of "lines of sight." The clack of shoes in empty rooms. Now he walked, his wife behind him, her words lost in another emptiness. He took in the furniture and appliances and shelved knickknacks but didn't feel their tug. He might as well have been walking across a stage set. He might as well have been walking on the moon.

Alice's voice: "Have you been drinking?"

"Jason?"

"Tell me what happened."

He paused at the stairway's base. A hand on the rail. A gathering of strength. A current broke over him. An avalanche of years and days and all he'd lost. A step, and with it, a wooziness. The car's motion still in him. He had a concussion, he was sure of it. He'd had them before, high school, college. The bell-ringers. The black flash. The whiff of smelling salts. Behind him, the bird call of Alice's voice, the chirp of questions, a language he couldn't understand without watching her mouth form the words. The upstairs hallway, and he paused outside their daughter's room. On her shut door, a collage. Ticket stubs, photos, magazine clippings—movie stars and boy bands. Charcoal images torn from her sketchbook. His finger on a fortune cookie's pink slip. *The best is yet to come.*

He turned on the shower and took off his clothes. Alice in the doorway. Her questions abandoned, and he stood naked before her. She picked up his sweatshirt and smoothed her hand over the stained sleeve, and when she stared into his eyes, all he could offer her was a hundred hollow miles. Beneath the light, curls of steam.

She gathered his clothes, a leap into action while he remained paralyzed. He heard her on the steps then pulled back the window's curtain. Below, the patio doors, Alice in the light's spill. A flicker before she scurried to the alley's trashcans.

Jason wiped the fogged mirror. His reflection clear then not. He stepped into the shower, and for a moment, he thought he'd swoon. The heat. The night's carousel of faces. Water filled his cupped palms. Ripples on the surface. He tried to lift his hands, but he couldn't. The weight. The disconnect between body and thought. He opened his hands, and the water splashed over his feet. He lowered himself and sat, elbows on his knees. The shower's stream stinging his neck.

* * *

He blinked himself awake. A dream of his stepfather's rowboat upon a wide lake, and in the hull, a carp. The fish flopping, its gaping mouth, the sun reflected in its black eyes. Morning light around the bedroom curtains. Alice, still in her flannels and sweatshirt, passed out next to him. Last night, he listened to her scrubbings, her treks back and forth to the garage and alley trash cans. He rested his nose against her forehead. On her, the bite of disinfectants. The hospital scent they knew so well.

They spoke over breakfast—what to be prepared for and the importance of appearances. They pushed aside their uneaten food and held hands. The prayers they'd once offered here replaced by this pact. The two of them against the world.

The morning's peculiar rhythms. His lack of sleep. The concussion's fog. His commute's landmarks infused with a new shine, and he donned his sunglasses despite the clouds. He turned into the corporate center. Last generation's farmland replaced by curving roads and low-slung office buildings—brick and glass, trees so carefully spaced Jason imagined the development as an architect's model. A world in miniature. He turned into one of the lots and claimed his reserved parking space.

Outside, and his coat's unbuttoned flaps lifted with the wind. A crow perched atop a light pole cawed then took to the sky. Behind the office, a row of naked trees, and between them, the flicker of highway traffic. In Jason, the sensation of drift, the knowing of this landscape yet being unclaimed by it. Everything slippery. Everything liquid. The door, his reflection across the glass' lettering—*Fulbright and Smith Personal Wealth Management*, and here, another disconnect. His job's shell game of capital begetting capital. The momentum of wealth. Jason knew his types—the hedgers and gamblers. The ones who didn't read their statements. The ones who called weekly, shifting funds, chasing ghosts.

"Happy Friday, Mr. Driscoll." Kathleen the receptionist handed him his mail. Her headset and ergonomic chair. On her desk, framed pictures, her sons in their graduation gowns and prom tuxedos.

He took the envelopes. "Thank you."

She set a card upon the desk's ledge, a glance to her left and right before handing him a pen. "It's Sherry's birthday."

He struggled to focus, the penned offerings of his office-mates twisting like minnows in shallow water. He signed, the simplest of greetings.

"There'll be cake in the breakroom later." She took the card. "Your head—"

"A little accident." He touched his forehead. "Looks worse than it feels."

She smiled. "I should see the other guy, right?"

Madison Baker joined them. She took the mail Kathleen offered. "What other guy?" She cocked her head, the lightness of morning banter replaced by concern. "Whoa. That's some bump."

"It's OK, really." He tucked his mail beneath his arm, but before he left, Kathleen called. "Mr. Driscoll?"

"Yes?"

"I have aspirin if you need it."

"Thank you, Kathleen."

Madison walked by his side. Black hair, a beige blazer. Her calves knotted by the trails she and her husband hiked. Between them, an unspoken attraction, the latent, slow-blos-soming kind common to workplaces. Their shared frustrations and common enemies. Their long hours. Neither were flirts, but he did like to make her smile. Her squint, a hand over her

11

mouth, her body's tremors as she suppressed the laugh she feared rang too loud. But this morning on the raised walkway that circled the pit, he felt her looking through him, and he shivered beneath his coat.

"So the story?" She pointed to her head. "Behind this?"

The walkway marked the office's perimeter, and off it, the offices of the associates and junior partners. Four steps below the walkway, the pit, the dozen-plus cubicles of the firm's agents. Years ago, Jason and Madison had formed an alliance in the pit. They shared tips and leads, talked each other up when they had a partner's ear. In the pit's center, a gathering at Nathan Zimmerman's cubicle. The young men laughing, hyenas at the waterhole, the privileged brotherhood that had seen their kind from the playground to the frat house. Nathan —the others called him Zimmy, but Jason refused—nodded as Jason and Madison passed. Nathan was the flash-talking, prep-school type Mr. Smith liked, no doubt because Nathan reminded him of his own jerky sons. Quarterly reports were the trust's lifeblood, and Nathan was the pit's rising star. Jason's own earnings had lagged these past six quarters, and while he'd been offered an unofficial grace period—the tragedy he'd endured, the whispers that still circulated behind his back—he knew Nathan and the pit's hyenas had their eyes upon him.

Madison spoke, a heads-up about a presentation they'd been tasked with giving, but her words faded beneath the pulse of fluorescents and computer screens. Jason unsure if the space between his ears was filled with helium or lead.

They paused outside his office door. "We'll catch up later about the presentation. No rush on that—we won't be doing it until the end of the quarter."

"OK." His hand on the doorknob. An anchoring. The sway in his body.

"You OK?"

"Nothing a little coffee won't cure." Nathan's cackle rose from the pit. "Thanks."

They made plans to talk over lunch, and inside his office, Jason leaned against his shut door. His briefcase and letters dropped to the floor. The swirl enveloped him. He closed his eyes. The carp in his stepfather's boat. This drowning in open air.

A fall Saturday. The leaves' last colors. Sun and blue skies. Jason and Alice walked through their neighborhood. Rabbits on the wide lawns. Squirrels. Marigolds in the flowerbeds, and soon, the first hard frost. The Andersons paused, rakes in hand. A honk from their daughter as she backed her car from the driveway. Hellos and small talk with her parents, but behind them, Jason saw his daughter, cartwheels across the grass. Saw her turning to wave from their porch. Her girlhood of pool parties, of birthdays and sleepovers.

Alice squeezed his hand. A kindness. A reassurance. Both of them tuned to the frequency beneath the Andersons' nods and half-smiles. Good neighbors like the Andersons didn't talk to Jason and Alice about sorrow—instead, they searched for it in their eyes. Polite voyeurs. The desire to gaze upon what scared them most.

They said their goodbyes, and Jason and Alice headed to Main Street. This gentrified stretch of boutiques and eateries. The ten miles to the streets of his youth may as well have been a hundred. A thousand. Another planet. His hand still in hers, but in him, a building revulsion. The memory of what his hands had done. The echo of snapped bone.

He let go, and with his other hand, he touched a light pole's yellow ribbon. Every pole with a ribbon, their tips lifted on the breeze. They claimed a table in a coffeeshop. At the register, a flier, the face that had stared at him across Flannigan's bar. Blond hair. A pink and purple windbreaker. The prayers of their town. A street of yellow ribbons. He ordered two cappuccinos and a slice of cherry pie.

Sunlight through the shop's windows. The shine upon their table and his folded hands. "Do you want to tell me about it?"

14

Alice asked. The sun upon her too, the lines of her face. The twenty-five years they'd been together. "Not now I mean but sometime?"

He unclasped his hands, the light cupped in his palms before he rested them upon his lap. "No."

She nodded. "I understand. But if you do—"

"If I do." A couple claimed the table behind her. The man set down a baby carrier. The baby's soft tears. The woman's coos.

"No word from anyone at work?" Jason asked. Jazz on the speakers. The espresso machine's hiss.

"There was some talk, but it's only been one day."

"They'll know. They'll know soon enough."

The barista called his name. Jason with the cappuccinos, Alice with the pie. The baby at the next table cried. The mother lifted her from the carrier. The girl's cheeks red, her face turned side to side as she refused her pacifier.

Alice's fork bothered the pie's crust. She leaned forward, her voice low. "The ones who were talking about it were assuming it was something with his ex or his son. But it doesn't seem real. Not with no one knowing and everyone going about their business."

Jason blew into his cup. The mother at the next table stood. She rocked her baby. Whispered sweet words. Still, the sobbing grew, and the pitch swelled in Jason's gut. He sipped then grimaced. The drink scalding, a heat he could barely swallow.

Alice's phone on the table, and she tapped it, checking the time. The screensaver a photo of her and Sophie, cheek to cheek, wide smiles. The eyes they shared. The screen faded and went dark. She took a bite of pie. Jason did the same, but the sweetness was lost beneath his tongue's burn. The baby cried, relentless, piercing. Her face over her mother's shoulder, an expression twisted and red and bloated. Jason closed his eyes.

A ding on Alice's phone. Then two more in quick succession. She bit her lip. Over the picture of her and Sophie, a string of texts. Shock. Disbelief. The baby wailed.

Jason stood. "Let's go." Their drinks and pie left on the table. Jason dizzy. The baby. The shop's clatter. Alice's dinging phone. The world crashing all around him.

* * *

Monday, and Jason, having forgotten to pack a lunch, considered the offerings of the breakroom's vending machines. He bought a water, a sleeve of cashews and raisins, but the corkscrew dispenser wedged his Cheez-Its against the display's glass. He tapped the window. In him, a lopsided anger. This bag—his life. He clutched the machine's sides and shook, and when the bag didn't budge, he slammed the glass with his palm. The bag fell, and when he retrieved it, he noticed Kathleen studying him. Her chair rolled back from her desk, a peek into the breakroom.

Jason claimed a bench by the parking lot. A cold front on the way, and with it, a breeze. The scuttle of clouds. Shadows and sun and tumbling leaves. Across the lot, a lawyer's office, an oral surgeon. The parking lot's long faces. Root canals and divorces. He could have eaten inside, but he was suffocating. The air that had been exhaled by a dozen others. The small talk. The copy machine's hum. The office's windows reflected the clouds, the glass as gray as his grandmother's blind eyes.

The clouds parted, and between them, a gasp of sun. He was grateful his grandmother had passed thinking he shared her faith. Her hope the sacred, burning heart of Jesus would eclipse his father's darkness. The Sundays he guided her down St. Mark's aisle. A hand on her elbow as she knelt. Her blindness freed him to daydream. The stained glass. The candles' flicker. The flowers placed at the Virgin's feet. Her expression of peace. Of eternity. The tide that lifted him when the congregation spoke in one voice. *Lord, have mercy. Christ, have mercy.*

She died the summer he turned eleven, and outside the occasional bout of guilt or existential malaise, Jason didn't think much of her beliefs, but with Sophie's diagnosis, he returned to

17

prayer. The words awkward at first, then easier. And as hope and his daughter faded, his prayers grew more impassioned. Their bedside vigils (*their* because Alice joined him, the two of them holding hands, their heads bowed, prayers to start the days and prayers to end them, prayers over the phone when the other was lost). Their desire to be close, to not let a single word or sigh go unwitnessed. Their need to be there to bring her water or pull back the curtain, to let her squeeze their hands against the pain. Most important, their need to not let her pass alone. Their lives narrowed. This choking point where only the essential mattered. Comfort. Breath. Their house. Her room. The wolf at the door, and when the end drew near, Jason allowed himself the comfort of embracing heaven. The fairy-tale reunion of paradise and an existence without suffering. He twisted the cap from his water bottle. He could still believe in heaven, but he could no longer imagine his place in it, and he considered the clouds that had reclaimed the sun, and he wondered what now. What now.

A yellow Mustang wheeled into the lot, a lap made before it claimed two spaces at the deserted end. Nathan Zimmerman climbed out. A look back before he hit the fob. A workout bag over his shoulder, his lunches spent at a strip-mall gym. Jason lifted the Cheez-It bag and shook the crumbs into his mouth. Nathan slid off his polarized Ray-Bans. "Didn't know you were the health-food type, J."

Jason's eyes narrowed. A sizing up, just as he'd done a hundred times on the mat. After his mother remarried and they moved out of the city, Jason came to know boys like Nathan. Boys who could flip the switch between manners and cruelty. Boys who wrecked their fathers' cars and walked away, unscratched and unrepentant. Boys who stopped listening to their teachers once they realized they'd one day earn triple their salaries. Boys who told stories about the girls they sweettalked into backseats and party-house bedrooms. Their fathers played golf and their mothers paid tutors to write their sons' college application essays, and together, they summered at the shore and wintered in Vail and Aspen. Wary of Jason's size, the bruises and black eyes he accumulated in football and wrestling, the boys allowed him distance, but Jason knew he'd never be one of them. This tribe who took nothing seriously beyond their own pleasure. Who'd never know what it was like to grow up hungry and afraid.

He wiped the crumbs off his lap. He wasn't up for banter, especially from Nathan. "Nope. Not a health-food nut."

Nathan readjusted his bag's strap. Perhaps he was waiting for Jason to offer a joke. Or perhaps the joke he was ready to offer wilted beneath Jason's stare. This silent declaration that Jason was done being civil to this little shit who wanted his job.

Jason and Alice joined the others in a church parking lot. Sunday afternoon, the believers given time to drive home and change into their jeans and hiking boots and down vests. Volunteers handed out granola bars and bottled water, and as Jason settled into the school bus that would take them to the state game lands, he looked out the dirty window and thought of his daughter's first day of kindergarten. A wave as the bus pulled away. A journey that was hers alone.

The bus chugged through town. Main Street's yellow ribbons, and in the country, they picked up speed. Sunlight flickered on the windows, and in Jason, a queasiness. The silence. The bus's sway and fumes. The rattle blurred the features of Alice's face, and beneath the surface, a deeper blur. An unraveling. Her dinnertime tears. Her sleepless nights. The skin she picked from her lips.

They parked on a packed-dirt trailhead. Another bus nearby, a trio of State Police cruisers. Jason and the others exited and gathered around a trooper who stood atop a boulder. The trooper spoke, a voice that reminded Jason of his old football coach. Gruff. Direct. A man accustomed to being listened to. They were here on a tip. If they found anything, they weren't to touch it. They'd walk a quarter mile into the woods. Along the way, they were to pick up a branch long enough to stir the leaves. A trooper with an orange flag would anchor each end of the line. They'd sweep up the hillside and meet the other search parties atop the summit.

Alice found a branch and, using her boot, snapped it into a walking stick. She picked up another, broke off a length, and handed it to Jason. Jason worried about the fitness of the others —the beer bellies, the slumped shoulders—but not Alice. He was stronger than her, but she was tougher, grittier. She'd proved it on their college's green fields, a team that never broke .500, her resolve to hustle through every whistle. Proved it in a bloody, drugless childbirth. Proved it day and night during Sophie's sickness. Her compassion and brave face. Her willingness to throw up her fists if a fight was what their daughter needed.

Their trek into the woods quiet. This somber business. Above, a thousand overlapping branches, and in the fractured light, darting finches, the last tumbling leaves. The path veined with roots. The hitch in his knee. The trooper in front blew his whistle, and the line halted. An officer in the rear spoke into a megaphone. He asked them to stand arm's length apart, then step back again. The line shuffled, separating here, closing there. Jason's arms raised. Alice beside him, their fingers touching, then—as she stepped back—not.

The whistle blew, and they left the path. The leaves deep. The crunch of boots. The line's order lost then found and lost again. Stumbles, the hidden rocks. The ever-steeper hillside. Boulders, some as big as cars, debris from a time this hill was entombed in ice. Jason waved his stick through the brush. The leaves shifted, the stir mesmerizing, and with each pass of his stick, a flash of pink and purple. A heartbeat. A mirage.

His phone buzzed. *Talk?*

Jason shut his office door, the view of the pit eclipsed. He settled into his chair and called Alice. "Hey."

"Hey," she said. Her tone off.

He swiveled in his chair, his back to the door. "Are the police there?"

"Yes."

"Are you at your desk?"

"Yes."

"We're good. We've practiced this. Right? Start rooting around. Get your keys." He heard voices, her office's comings and goings. "Do you have your keys?"

"I do."

"Go out to the car. Leave your coat."

"OK."

"Take a breath. You're just checking something in the car." His words calm, even. "If anyone asks, it's my wallet."

He listened, an aside. "My husband," she said. "He thinks he left his wallet in my car. I'll be right back."

"Tell me when you're outside." He imagined her office, a parallel universe. Breakroom snacks and signed birthday cards. He thought of Fast Eddie, their daughter's hamster, the ceaseless creak of its wheel. His little heart and the miracle it didn't explode.

"I'm out."

"You're doing fine." He pictured the breeze in her hair, her body tightening against the cold. "Did you park on the side or in the front?"

"Side."

"So someone might be able to look out and see you?"

"They could if they were at a window."

"Go to the car. Get in the passenger side and pretend to look in the glove."

The beep of her fob. The wind's hiss died when she settled in. "OK."

"What's it like?"

"They're bringing people into the conference room. One at a time. There are two of them. Detectives. A man and a woman."

"What are the people they've talked to saying?"

"Jimmy said it was mainly outside of work things. His ex. Their son. They wanted to know things Roger talked about. If he had any enemies."

"Keep looking. Glove. Console." He paused. "I've never told you about that night, right? I never told you anything. I'll never tell you, and as long as I never tell you, you'll never know what happened."

"Jason—"

"You'll never know. Say it. Say 'I don't know.'"

"I don't know." Her voice weak. The crunch of leaves.

"Say it again."

"I don't know."

"Again."

"I don't know."

"And when you go back, you'll smile and shake your head and make a joke about how absentminded I am. How I found my wallet in my coat pocket while you were looking."

"I'm at the door now."

"You don't know anything about that night. It's the truth."

"I don't know a thing."

His heart drummed, and he thought of Fast Eddie, his little grave behind their shed. His body dug up by the neighbor's dog, a secret they kept from Sophie. "Alice?"

"Yes?"

"We can see this through."

"I know."

"I love you."

"I know. I know."

Jason cinched the trash bag as Alice loaded the dishwasher. He put on his coat and slid back the patio doors. His breath silver in the moonlight. The scurry of cats as he approached the trashcans. Over dinner, he and Alice had discussed her interview. Her time in the conference room no longer than the others. The woman, Detective Norman, asked most of the questions. Her phone on the table and everything recorded. Questions about Roger's divorce. About his son, a boy lost in the haze of drugs. Alice admitted she didn't know much about his personal life, then the offhand remarks she and Jason had rehearsed. The investments Roger hinted at, his dreams to retire early and move somewhere where it never snowed. Watercooler talk, she told the detectives. Pipedreams.

He closed the patio doors behind him. The cold on his cheeks. The kitchen's warmth and the dishwasher's hum. Alice in her coat and gloves. "Ready?" she asked.

How pretty, their neighborhood this time of year. Homes outlined in strings of white, trees ablaze. The lights put up by contractors, this new service. Blocks that looked like movie sets. The first half of their walk silent before Alice spoke. "This time last year, I didn't think I could go on."

A car pulled into a driveway. The house's front door swung back, a woman in a lit doorway. The car's back doors opened, and a pair of children in karate gis ran up the sidewalk. This would be Jason and Alice's third Christmas without Sophie, and after they buried her, the bills came—or, more correctly, they'd been coming all along, but without the distraction of hope, they became real. How different, the worlds of insurers and healers. They cashed in Sophie's college fund, the stocks Jason had inherited from his stepfather. If he'd been a client,

Jason would have told himself to consider selling their house. Its value had doubled since they purchased it, the space they no longer needed. But Jason never brought it up. His fear of leaving this place. Of losing the background of his memories. Of losing Sophie again.

Later that year, one of Alice's internal audits raised a suspicion about the procedures in Roger Cormac's office. She assumed it was a mistake, a glitch when they shifted software platforms, and instead of reporting it, she talked to Roger first. Roger had been through his own troubles, and Alice's wounded heart recognized its echo in his. Their conversation in the privacy of her office. Her printouts spread upon her desk. She'd expected some kind of sloppiness, a lack of protocol, the forms he'd neglected, but then her shock when Roger broke down and admitted his years-long embezzlement. A plan simple and ingenious, the snagging of crumbs between shuttled accounts. A quarter million dollars, a sum Roger tearfully promised to replace. Or, he proposed, there was another option.

Alice and Jason discussed the matter that evening. He agreed she'd have to turn him in, but the more they talked, the more the idea of a missing quarter million, a sum not brazenly stolen but leaked out in dribbles and sighs, turned abstract. Alice's hedging a kind of asking, and when Jason said yes, it was less about the money than the belief they were owed. That the time had come to grab something from the world that had taken so much.

They passed the house of Sophie's best friend. A wreath on the door. Beth's bedroom window dark, the girl off at her first year of college. "There's a note," Jason said. "It's in my toolbox, under the top tray's rubber mat. I want you to give it to the police if something would happen to me."

She stopped. The house's pretty lights lifted her from the shadows. Steam from her lips. "What do you mean?"

"If something would happen—"

"What do you mean?" She took his gloved hand in hers. "I can't do this without you. I can't lose you. I can't be alone with all this."

A woman with a large dog appeared. Jason and Alice rejoined their walk. The dog old and slow, a sag in its leash. The woman with a knit cap and earbuds. A smile as she passed.

Jason waited then spoke. "All I've ever wanted to do was provide. For you. For our family. For my mother. I wanted to give you someplace safe. I need to know I'm giving you that. If this whole thing falls apart, I need to know that. The note takes the blame for everything. You're left out. You'll be able to keep the house. You'll be able to—"

"Please," she said. "No more. Not now."

Later, he waited for her in bed. Moonlight on the window, and in the dark, he thought of his letter. The words a period to all he knew and loved. The desire to die rather than rot in jail, and with the notion, a kind of peace. Alice emerged from the bathroom. The light behind her, her face lost, but beneath her sheer top, her body's silhouette. She turned off the light and settled beside him.

She kissed him, long and slow. Years ago, they'd exchanged vows, the life they promised to share, and here, in this kiss, a new life. Their fates bound by secrets and blood. The disconnect of his past days fell away, and in its place a tide that lifted him to her and this moment. The sea grew around them. Their shattered hearts and the things they'd done. This bed an island, and he clung to her, desperate, needing her like never before.

* * *

Upstate, and the two-lane road twisted through the woods. Browns and grays, and beneath the branches, a stubborn mist. Four years had passed, yet the route came back to him, its hills and turns, the towns with their general stores and two-pump gas stations. The Romans feared the German forests. The dead and their spirits. The slaughter at Teutoburg. Jason remembered lying awake in his stepfather's cabin and how the woods changed at night. The currents that drifted through the window screens. The pulse of cicadas and crickets and hooting owls.

He missed the spur. A U-turn, and at the wood's edge, a buck, a wide rack and black eyes, a moment of recognition before its bounding retreat. The spur gravel and dirt. He unhooked the chain that sagged between the posts he'd helped his stepfather dig. In the trunk, a chainsaw, but the path, while overgrown, was free from fallen trees, and he parked in the cabin's clearing. Bill—his stepfather and the man Jason would come to call Dad—had brought Jason here not long after he married Jason's mother. At the cabin, Jason shot a .22 and gutted fish. He smelled the pines after summer rains. He lit bonfires, and the sparks rose to a sky of more stars than he'd ever imagined.

Bill was a man of great kindness and few words, and in time, Jason came to understand both Bill's and the cabin's silence. There was a comfort in saying nothing, in giving over to the push of wind in the trees and the hiss of cast lines. Jason had brought Sophie here. Day trips—her love of the lake and her grandfather but not the cabin, its spiders, its outhouse. Before Bill died, he offered Jason the cabin, and he smiled, his thumb on his morphine drip, perhaps remembering their time

28

together. Jason said yes, of course, but after Bill passed, Jason realized he couldn't maintain the property. His commitments, Sophie's soccer, the two-hour drive. Instead, he offered the cabin to one of Bill's nephews, the deal marked with a handshake and the invitation for Jason to return anytime.

He exited his car. Colder here. The pines the only remnant of summer's greens. The clearing's frosted slope to the lake. The lake wide, its center deep. The opposite shore shrouded in mist. The cabin's porch boards squeaked. The key fished from his coat pocket. Dim inside, the must of uncirculated air. The chairs empty, and Jason thought about Bill and how, one by one, they all left each other. He took the pair of wooden oars leaning against the hearth and stepped outside.

The frost crunched beneath his boots. The slope's grass recently cut, and he was glad Bill's nephew was looking after the place, glad someone was fending off the forest's creep. The turned-over rowboat lay near the water's edge. The boat old, wooden, the same boat Bill had rowed to his favorite fishing spots. The shaded pools. The lilies that draped the lifted paddles. Jason stooped and, with a grunt, turned the boat over, lurching back as the grass shivered with fleeing mice.

He set the oars in the boat, and from the car, he retrieved the laptop he'd stashed beneath the passenger seat. The laptop's lid scratched where Jason had razored off Roger's *Margaritaville* and *Mile o* stickers. He set the laptop in the hull and dragged the boat to the water's edge. The lake's mist stirred as a flock of geese took to the sky. Their honks and flapping wings. A balancing act, the boat meeting the water, his careful boarding. He used an oar to push off and, in a breath, was released from the physics of solid land.

He secured the oars into their locks. His back to the lake and the cabin receding. The rhythm awkward at first but then rising from his muscles. The mist heavier on the lake, and soon, he was alone with the boat's lurch, its creak and splash. In him, memories of other rhythms, his recent nights with Alice. How they'd moved and swore and begged. How they clung to each other as they wrestled at the edge of the world.

At the lake's middle, he pulled up the oars. The boat drifted then stopped. He thought of the frigid day he'd brought Sophie here to skate and her questions about the fish and how they lived beneath the ice. He blew into his numb hands and retrieved the screwdriver from his coat pocket. He removed the laptop's hard drive then stabbed it with the screwdriver. The tip brought down again and again until he felt a breaking inside the case. He tossed the hard drive into the water, rowed another thirty yards, and slipped the laptop over the side.

He drifted for a bit then put his oars in the water and rowed. He glanced back, lost for a moment, not certain where he was. Neither shore visible through the fog.

* * *

He lay beside Alice. Their ragged breath. His heart's slow unwind. His sweat and the room's chill. The whispering sex of parenthood behind them, this sad freedom. He listened to the furnace. Listened to the wind's hiss beneath the eaves. They'd fucked more in the past two weeks than they had in the previous two years. Daily, sometimes more, each time digging a little deeper. Finding themselves in the other's desperation. They had their history. The passions that gave way to familiarity. The rhythms Sophie had brought. The exhaustion of their jobs. The sorrow of two miscarriages and their decision to quit trying and carve a life from this rock, just the three of them.

Alice pulled the sheet over her breasts. "Know what I could use?" She pantomimed holding a cigarette, a long exhale.

He smiled. She'd smoked when they were dating—not much, her need to maintain her wind for sports, but sometimes she lit up at parties, a beer in one hand and a cigarette in the other. Then more after graduation, a smoke with her morning coffee, another after sex. "Too bad you promised not to."

She mimicked another toke. "Remind me why I did a stupid thing like that."

"Because I asked you to when we got married. Because I didn't want to think of you getting sick when we got old."

"I guess I should thank you for that."

"You should."

"But right now—" She took another imaginary puff then curled into him. In five minutes, she was asleep. She rolled over when Jason slid his arm from beneath her, but she didn't wake. He dressed, flannels, a sweatshirt. He couldn't sleep, not yet. Each day distanced him from that night in Roger's garage, yet

31

he kept circling back. The memory—yet also, the rendition of the memory, a portrait he kept filling in. The picture's boundaries blurring. Its colors more and more vivid.

He went downstairs. The quiet as deep as it was upon the lake. He filled a glass at the tap. His dry throat and the water cool. He lifted a picture from the wall. A child's drawing, their house, three windows, three waving people. He returned the picture. Sophie's death wasn't a single event, a period after the surrender of her exhausted heart. Her last breath radiated into the-all-and-everything of this life, a state of matter he couldn't comprehend or predict because sometimes she was lost and other times she came alive in a million reflections, in passing conversations and radio snippets, in the scurry of playground children. There were days he drowned in her memory—and other days he drowned without her—and if he had to choose, he'd rather be haunted than abandoned. Anything to keep from losing her again.

He stood before the patio doors. His reflection in the glass undercut by a kind of static. He slid back the door and stepped outside. The cold upon him, and from the sky, the season's first flurries.

* * *

Jason's mail waited on Kathleen's desk. Her chair abandoned, but her voice carried from the break room. A glimpse as he passed. The arrangement of muffins, a banner hung. Another birthday.

In the pit, Nathan cradled his phone against his collarbone. His fingers' meaty keyboard clack. Fifteen minutes until the day's official start, yet Nathan and the other go-getters were already riding their caffeine buzz. The hope to be noticed. To shine. To be lifted from the pit. Mr. Smith's secretary stepped from the corner office. "Mr. Driscoll?" When Jason neared, she lowered her voice. "Mr. Smith would like to see you. Someone's with him." She leaned closer and whispered: "From the police. About a client."

She shut the office's door behind him and claimed her seat. Jason remained standing. A schoolboy's pose. He filled his lungs, the deep breathing he'd used before a match. The knowing he was in for a fight. The secretary hung up the phone. "You can go in now, Mr. Driscoll."

Jason had always found the light in David Smith's corner office unsettling. His boss reduced to shadows while David squinted. The windows that followed the sun from morning to afternoon. The glint off plaques and framed photos of David Smith shaking hands with politicians and athletes. Jason remembered the morning he told Smith his daughter was starting hospice. Jason's tearing eyes unable to focus in this room of sparkle and glare. His composure's slow unravel. A feeling like he was falling into a cold, cold sun.

A woman occupied the place where he'd sat that day, and when he entered, she stood. Brown hair that touched her shoulders, brown eyes that looked into his. Black slacks and a black

33

blazer—an appearance little different than any other woman in the office, but when she shook his hand, her blazer pulled aside to reveal her holstered gun.

"Jason, this is Detective Norman. She's here to talk about your work with Mr. Cormac."

"Yes, we heard about that." Jason let go of her hand. "It's terrible news."

He'd been preparing himself—the police, their questions—and in his heart, the fear a detective's trained eye would see through his lies. He thought of his last hours at Sophie's bedside, thought of the scuffle in Roger's garage—and here he was again, the whole of his life funneling to this moment and the ground upon which he stood.

Mr. Smith offered the detective the firm's full cooperation then asked Jason to take her to his office. Jason led the way. The eyes of the pit lifted, all of them hyenas, the scent of blood. The detective smiled when Jason said not all the offices were as nice as his boss's, and in him, the calm that once found him when a ref blew his whistle. The roar of fieldhouses and gyms erased by his thudding heart, and even though this woman represented the system and all its brutality, Jason found peace in knowing there'd be no ambiguity between them. No networking. No social climbing. No backscratching. There would only be the truth and Jason's struggle to keep her from it.

He offered the detective a seat and shut his office door. In his thoughts, a filter, the imagining of a man with a clear conscience. Helpful, surprised, but in the end, indifferent. She declined his offer of water or coffee and flipped to a new page in her notepad.

"So how can I help you, Detective Norman?"

"We're examining Mr. Cormac's affairs, and we wanted to see if you could shed some light." She clicked her pen. "How would you describe your relationship?"

Jason retrieved Roger Cormac's file from his cabinet and set it on the desk. "Mr. Cormac came to us about a year ago." He opened the file. "A year and a month." He closed the file. "I'm not sure what I'm allowed to share with you."

"The executor of Mr. Cormac's estate has given us permission to make inquiries on his holdings."

Jason nodded. "Then what can I tell you?"

"How much did he come to you with initially?"

Jason checked his paperwork. "About three hundred thousand. There were a couple accounts he drew together."

"Did that amount raise any red flags?"

"No. We handle some rather large accounts."

"Did he transfer his funds from another planner?"

"No. Most of his holdings seemed to have been squirreled away in various low-risk accounts. He also cited a recent inheritance."

"Was any of this uncommon?"

"It wasn't typical, but there are all kinds of investor profiles. He came off as a more conservative type, at least in our first meetings."

"And then?"

"Then he wanted to diversify. Parcel some things out. Try to get a little more return. Be a little more aggressive."

She jotted something in her notepad. "We became curious after seeing his cellphone records. He called here a number of times, especially during the last two months."

Jason's hands in his lap, his tension channeled into a hidden grip. "He did."

"And what were those conversations like?"

"He suddenly had a lot of questions. Concerns. One day it was one thing, the next it was something else."

"Did you keep notes of these calls?"

Alice and Sophie smiled from his desk's framed picture.

His stepfather's cabin. The lake behind them, and in the water, the forest's reflection, the leaves at their brightest. "Most, yes."

She looked up from her pad. "But not all?"

"Mr. Cormac was . . . well, he grew rather concerned. He kept circling around to the same topics. To be honest, I found myself doing a lot of repeating. And reassuring."

She clicked her pen. "Would you say he was nervous?"

Jason let her question hang. His role demanded generosity. Diplomacy. "Some clients invest and we only speak at our yearly reviews. Others are more . . . involved."

"And what was the gist of these conversations?"

"They often revolved around how fluid his funds were. How quickly he could cash out if he wanted to. He alluded a number of times to an investment. An opportunity to get on the ground floor of something. Something he thought might make him a lot of money."

Her pen scratched across the pad. "Did he elaborate?"

"Something to do with real estate. But he wasn't very specific."

"Did any of this seem suspicious? Did he come off as agitated in any way?"

"He didn't talk much about his home life, but I got the impression things weren't great." He paused, and the muscles in his clenched hands eased. "Perhaps he was a little agitated. At least in our last few calls." He shrugged. "But I didn't think much of it at the time. That's just how some people are with their money."

* * *

He passed the store every day. A Pizza Hut on one side, a minimart on the other. A plate-glass front, and curbside, an electric sign, a stream of repeated messages. *Concealed Carry Classes. Cigar Bar. We Back the Blue.* A bell rang as Jason stepped inside. Music and bright displays, a layout that reminded him of his daughter's favorite stores at the mall. Only here, there were guns. Guns everywhere he looked.

And as it had in Anthropologie and American Apparel, his vocabulary abandoned him. Rifle and handgun, blouse and skirt—he understood these but not the hundred nuances that made one different than another. He walked down an aisle. Black guns. Camouflage guns. Silver ones that held his passing reflection. Pink guns. A father pulled a rifle from a display, gazed down its sights, and handed it to his son. A woman posed for a selfie in front of a stuffed bear, the bear standing, its paws stretched wide. Jason thought about these people—and he thought about Flannigan's soggy booths and the man who could have been his father—and he saw the world splintered into a series of secret universes. The overlap of far-flung orbits, the lonely centers reserved for the faithful. The true believers.

A nametag identified the man approaching him as *Roger.* Jason blinked and the letters rearranged into *Randy.* Randy wore the sales staff's blue polo, the shop's name emblazoned over his heart. The material stretched over his stomach, a pinch at his neck, and he reminded Jason of the grandfatherly types common to hardware stores and barber shops. The store lights shone on his bald spot and oversized glasses. "What can I help you with today, young man?"

"I'm looking for a gun. A handgun."

"Any specific purpose?" Randy's smile lingered into the

37

silence he'd expected Jason to fill. His tone turned gentle, as if he were talking to a child. "Target? Home protection?"

"Home protection."

"For you? Your wife?"

"Me. Just me."

"Do you own any firearms?"

"No." He thought of the cabin, Bill's long-barreled .22, the ping of bottles and cans.

"Let me show you some beauts that might do the trick."

Jason followed him to a display case. On the walls, muted TVs, men and women on a firing range, hunters perched in tree stands. Some guns nestled beneath the display's glass. Others posed atop stands and tethered by plastic-sheathed chains.

Randy laid three guns atop the glass. He spoke as he performed a check of their magazines and chambers. "What kind of men would we be if we let the evil of the world into our homes?"

Jason stared at the guns. "Yes."

Randy handed Jason the first gun. Black, a hard plastic grip. Its weight surprising. "All of these are compact and easy to use. And more importantly, each has stopping power." He started giving the second gun's specs when Jason interrupted him. "This one." He handed back the gun he'd been holding. "This is the kind I was thinking about."

Randy smiled. "The man knows what he likes. And I must say that's my first choice too." He put the other guns back and locked the case. "Would you like to test it before we get to the paperwork? We have a range downstairs."

Jason followed him. A door in the rear, and on its other side, the store's polish disappeared. Wooden stairs and cinderblock walls. The space windowless and bare. A sign: *Welcome to the bunker!* Below, a list of rules: *Treat every gun as if it was loaded. Keep all guns pointed downrange. Keep fingers outside trigger guard until you're ready to fire.* The ceiling low, the floor open and as long as a bowling alley. At their end, four booths, all empty. Target in hand, Randy walked to the floor's other end. His shoes clacked, echoes off the low ceiling. The target a scowling man, his pistol aimed straight ahead.

Randy gave Jason a pair of safety glasses and donned his own. "Have you ever fired a weapon?"

"A rifle. A .22. A long time ago."

"This is a different beast." He slid out the magazine and loaded three bullets. "This is going to have a bit of a kick, so get ready for that." He demonstrated a two-handed grip. "Important thing is to be calm. Steady yourself, make sure everything is where it should be, then slide your finger into the guard and squeeze."

He donned a pair of padded earmuffs and handed a pair to Jason. "Ready?" he asked. He handed over the gun, and when Jason aimed it, Randy gave his hands a slight adjustment. He flicked the safety and stepped back. "You're hot."

Jason looked down the sights. A cartoon enemy of black and white. If he ever fired the gun, it would be a single shot. A real-life period to childhood games of cops and robbers, good guys and bad.

Randy's voice called from a distant shore. "Just breathe and squeeze."

The supermarket on a Tuesday evening. Music on the speakers, songs from Jason's youth. The demographic bullseye upon his wallet. He pushed the cart while Alice scanned the shelves. Around them, a hundred bright colors. An old man passed. Shuffling steps, an oxygen pack, clear tubing over his ears and beneath his nose. In his cart, cat food, frozen dinners. Alice checked her list and set a can of tomato paste in the cart, and for a moment, their eyes met. This sober recognition. Their hopes of salvation buried beneath their sins, and nothing remained but survival. The two of them alone in the wilderness.

The cart's wheel squeaked as they turned into the produce aisle. This sea of greens and reds and yellows. A mother by the apples, a little girl in the cart's seat. Juicebox slurps, an unzipped coat, and both Alice and Jason paused. The old man with the oxygen pack weighed bananas. His hands shook as he tore one from the bunch and weighed them again. Jason's foot tapped in time with a song he used to play in his first car. Alice held a honeydew in each hand, lifting, judging. She turned her back to the old man and held the honeydews before her breasts, a jiggle and a grin before setting them in the cart. Jason smiled, but beneath, he thought about prison. Another kind of wilderness. A life without color. Without whim or will. A landscape that would swallow him and his memory.

He helped bag at the checkout. At each register, a flier. The girl in a purple and pink jacket. The blue eyes that never blinked. The register beeped, a gum-chewing teen, the ballet of her hands. The honeydews shimmied on the belt. Between the cashier's lips, a pink bubble, a swell, a tiny pop.

In the lot, Jason loaded the groceries then claimed the

passenger seat. Alice started the car, but before she shifted into reverse, he placed his hand over her breast. He thought of Sophie, how she'd latch and nurse. The delicate suckling. The wetness on her lips. He thought of the life that had flowed from Alice's body, a miracle he'd understood but never fully comprehended. He thought of prison's ashy light, its madness and tears. The old man with the oxygen tank started the car next to theirs. Jason stared into Alice's eyes as his hand slid beneath her shirt, his touch soft then not. Her lips parted, a gasp. "Drive around back," he said.

She pulled from their space. His hand now between her legs. Rubbing, squeezing, and she jerked to a stop at the lane's end. Behind the store, a coatless worker threw cardboard bundles into a dumpster before hurrying inside. Jason nodded toward the lot's shadowed edge. "Over there."

She parked. In the car, the faintest of lights, blacks and grays. He unbuttoned his jeans and slid them down. He cupped the back of her neck, his fingers in her hair. He nudged her forward. She smiled, and her hesitation only made him want her more. He pulled, harder than before, and she slipped into the shadows.

* * *

Jason waited as Madison parked a few spaces away. Her door swung open, a delay as she gathered her things. He thought of their Richmond trip last year. A difficult client, a tangle of documents and a poisoned family history. A late-night unwinding in a hotel bar, and from her, confessions. The car crash that took her brother. The husband whose touch changed after they discovered they couldn't have children. Outside her room, both of them a little tipsy, he'd almost kissed her, not out of lust or pity, but from a kind of kinship, all of them in pain, all of them with their masks. He was thankful they'd parted with a simple *goodnight,* yet the memory of that hallway moment lingered. A tenderness. The desire to hold her and whisper the sweetest lie that everything would be OK.

She cursed, reached back into the car, and when he stepped closer, Jason noticed her boot. "Whoa, whoa," he said. He took her briefcase and purse.

"Thanks," she said. "It's already been a shit morning."

"Broken?" he asked.

She wrangled her laptop case and hobbled forward. "Fractured. In two places. Clumsy." The wind blew her hair across her face, and she tucked the wayward strands behind her ear. Their slow plod across the lot. "Missed a step. I heard it. Wasn't pretty."

Jason's grip tightened on her briefcase's handle. A shiver that had nothing to do with the cold. Madison stopped. "Shit. Forgot some files. Hold on."

"Hit the fob. I'll get them."

"Keys are in my purse."

He opened her purse and let her fish for the keys. Her car

lights winked. She called after him. "On the passenger seat. It's a mess. Don't judge me."

The car smelled of her shampoo. A leash on the floor, the chihuahua she loved, its picture on her desk. He retrieved the files. "Let's go, Hopalong."

The breeze kicked up. "You should have seen me navigating the shower."

Inside, and Kathleen rose from the desk. Sympathy, concern. Offers to help. The aspirin she kept in her desk. Madison smiled. "Thanks. I appreciate it."

Jason whispered as they walked off: "That's just the start, you know. You should've come up with a more interesting story than missing a step."

"When I was in the ER, this was the moment I was dreading. The attention. The blah-blah-blah of it."

The pit's gatherings paused as Jason and Madison passed. Nathan's fingers flexed, another squeaking rep of his handgrip. "What did the brute do to you, Madison?" Another rep, a grin when he spotted the purse over Nathan's shoulder.

She repositioned her laptop's strap. "I'd give you a hundred bucks to take a dive right now so I could hobble off unnoticed."

"Should've made that offer a little earlier." He opened her office door. "I could use a little extra cash flow."

He plugged in her laptop. Poured water into her coffeemaker and brewed her a cup. "I could survey the breakroom. Come back with the day's baked goods."

"No thanks. A few less grazings might be the one good thing to come of this." She lowered herself into her chair. "The files you brought in—can you hand them over?" He did, and she spoke as she thumbed through them. "How's your quarter looking?"

"Steady, but not stellar."

"You've had some tough luck. That Phelps ruling. And the

Johnson affair. Who could have predicted that?"

Unsaid, his other miscalculations. His lack of enthusiasm during their last retreat's team-building exercises. The plane he'd missed in Detroit and the subsequent two-day layover in the airport hotel as he waited out a blizzard. The cloud he'd carried these past two years. "Just got these." She handed him a pair of folders. "Why don't you make the calls? I'm behind with that whole Robertson thing. And now with this hoof."

She cited doctors' visits. Physical therapy. Excuses for a deeper kindness. He thanked her and told her to call if she needed anything. Outside her door, he removed one of her hairs from his sleeve. The strand pinched, and in the pit, Nathan watched. Another squeeze of his handgrips.

Jason shut his office door. Hung up his coat. A flashing red light on his desk's phone. He entered his code and listened. "Mr. Driscoll, this is Detective Norman. Can you return my call when you get this message?"

The message played three times, a sifting, her words, her tone. His hand shook as he wrote her number. A series of deep breaths before he called, and he was thankful it went to voicemail. His day spent worrying. Rationalizing. Imagining himself led out in handcuffs. His body engaged in workday rhythms—meetings and phone calls—his mind on another shore. His lunch uneaten. On the way home, he picked up his gun. A handshake from Randy. The gun on the passenger seat, a plastic case, a nesting of foam. A complimentary box of ammo and a pocket copy of the Constitution.

Rush hour during winter's early dark. This ugly stretch. Traffic lights every fifty yards. Strip malls. Chain restaurants. Gas stations and car dealers. Inflatable tube figures and their jerking dances. In the right lane, crawling semis, the spew of diesel. Cars jockeyed between the semis, and as the next light turned red, a black pickup swerved into Jason's lane. A slam of brakes, Jason's front end inches from the pickup's bumper. The pickup rumbled. The poison of its exhaust. In Jason's head, another poison, the chuff from Roger's lips as their tangled bodies struck the concrete. Their arms around each other. A pose of lovers. The warmth so real Jason brushed his ear.

The light changed. A belch of smoke, and the pickup cut into the other lane. Jason's radio off. The silence he needed to think. The posing and picturing of self. The awkwardness of his character upon a high school stage, memories of playing with Sophie and her dolls. The narrative of what could be. Then another imagining, the detective waiting at his house. A warrant. Alice broken, their secrets confessed. The light ahead turned red, and the black pickup veered back in front of him. Jason hit the brakes, and in his exasperation, beeped his horn.

The pickup's cab light shone as the driver jumped out. A burly man. A sweatshirt and baseball cap. His angry gestures captured in Jason's headlights. A clenched fist. A raised middle finger. Jason's exit a reflex. The stepping outside one's self when the irritation of the external world rose to match the internal. Beside them, the yellow glow of McDonald's arches. When the man in the cap took a step forward, Jason took two. Traffic zipped by on the other side of the median, and carried in the gusts, paper scraps, an eye-stinging grit. Jason not scared —quite the opposite. He felt liberated, anxious, his fists clenched and heavy as hammers. Backseat children stared from the car beside them.

The man in the baseball cap didn't move. "Watch who you're beeping at, cuz."

Jason said nothing. Between them, a glittering path, pebbles of glass and plastic. In his chest, a wild heart and a thousand coiled springs. He wanted the man to come at him. Wanted resolution. The light turned green. The semis in the right lane shuddered and crept forward. More faces behind glass. Then a complaint of horns. The man in the cap returned to his pickup and sped off.

The phone was ringing when Jason climbed back into his car. On the display, the number he'd called earlier. He shifted into drive, and with a button push, he accepted the call. "Hello."

"Mr. Driscoll, this is Detective Norman. Am I calling at a good time?"

"Yes. I'm in my car if that's OK."

"I don't want you to be distracted. Perhaps—"

"I'm fine. I'm on 15. In town." He was strangely calm, his adrenaline fading. "You know how it is this time of night. I'm doing more sitting than driving."

"Would you rather talk later?"

The black pickup barreled through a yellow light, and Jason rolled to a stop. "No. Please. I tried to return your call earlier."

"If you find yourself distracted—"

"I'll let you know."

"When we spoke the other day I hadn't made the connection that your wife worked with Mr. Cormac."

Jason had been prepared for this. "That's how we met. She introduced us."

"I'm surprised this didn't come up when we first spoke."

"I'm sorry. I should have mentioned it. It's just that my dealings with him and his account were so much more involved than our initial meeting."

"Can you describe that first meeting?"

Passing lights angled into his car. The gun case deep in the shadows. "It was at one of my wife's work events. A company picnic."

"Anything outside of that?"

"When he reached out about his portfolio, I made a house

call. He had some questions."

"Do you extend that courtesy to all your clients?"

"No, but there was something going on with him. I can't remember what—something with his car or his wife. Or with his son. But whatever it was, it was no big deal going over. He didn't live terribly far. His portfolio wasn't extraordinary, but it was a nice foundation. It had potential."

"But I got the impression he wasn't the long-haul type. The kind of guy eyeing sixty-five."

For a wrestler, a feint could be just as important as an attack. The planting of doubt. The questioning of balance. "He was. At first. But he changed."

"Did he seem like he was under duress?"

She was repeating herself now. He had to be careful. "He was always a little nervous."

"Did he ever talk like he was being pressured?"

Another red light, and Jason rolled to a stop. He lifted the case's latches and opened the lid. His fingers traced the gun's barrel. "Maybe. It's hard to say. Maybe if there was any pressure, it was coming from him. He kicked himself a lot. He kept going back, talking about how he should have invested differently. The chances he missed. And his focus became less long-term and more . . ." He paused, wanting to deliver his line with the right emphasis, "more immediate."

"You said he talked about other business dealings."

"Yes, but they were always vague. Or perhaps he was just being vague with me."

"Did he ever mention the reasons for withdrawing a series of large sums those last months? There's one for twenty-five thousand and another for thirty."

"I asked." Jason reached the strip's last light, and when it changed, he jockeyed his way forward. "But I never got a straight answer."

* * *

That evening, he and Alice sat at the dining room table and revisited their story. A timeline both fact and fiction. A script repeated until it became a hazy truth. Jason assured Alice he'd handled his call with the detective, but he was uneasy. The detective's tone. The knowing she'd heard the lies of a hundred guilty men. He had to be careful. He had to think right.

Voices from their yard, and on their windows, a flashlight's sweep. Alice grasped his hand. Their neighbor's dog had escaped again. The dog always running off, chases that devolved into tauntings of its frazzled owners. The same dog that had dug up Fast Eddie. Jason went on: "She knows about the money. The twenty-five and thirty thousand. Did she bring that up with you?"

"No. What did she say?"

"Nothing beyond that. For all she knows, it's buried in his yard." On the table, the day's mail. Another letter from their insurance company. Their daughter kept alive in figures and debts and veiled threats. The balance they didn't dare pay off all at once, even though they now could. "And there's no one looking at the books at your place?"

"No. They'd have to go back years. He covered his tracks, and I made sure to lose some key reports. And with the change in software, it would be even harder to find."

"And you remember my note? Just in case?"

She let go of his hand. "In the toolbox."

They startled. At the patio door, the neighbor's dog, a black and white terrier. The dog on its hind legs, its front paws scratching the glass. A moment's begging before it bound off, their neighbor and his flashlight giving chase.

Jason and Alice ate, cold leftovers, and later, as Alice showered, he knelt in the back of their bedroom closet. The carpet pulled back to expose the hiding place he'd cut into the floorboards. He groped, the space dark, and pulled out the cash box. Green metal, a sticker with his daughter's name, the box she'd used for summer lemonade stands. He counted out ten thousand, a sum he figured could buy him a new start. He listened to make sure the shower was still running. He'd snuck up the gun case and then wedged in the bills and secured the latch. Outside, his neighbor's voice, a barking dog. Jason set the gun case and metal box in the hiding place and replaced the floorboards.

The shower turned off. Jason went to the window. In the yard, his neighbor, a grip on the dog's collar, a tug of war. Jason undressed and sat on the bed's edge. The room dark save the slivers of light around the bathroom door. He listened, Alice's movements a fine thread beneath the hush. He stared into his empty hands. Wanting her. Needing her.

* * *

J ason grunted out his last rep and lowered the stack. He
stayed at the machine, the warm ache in his body, and
caught his breath. This his first workout since the night in
Roger's garage. The gyms of his youth different. His team-
mates' basements. The Y. Locations Spartan, the stink of sweat
and Lysol. The clang of metal. His college gym different. The
glittering fitness center built to attract students. It's sunlight
and modern machines. Its women. The one woman he'd marry,
his first glimpse on a treadmill, a workout she later confessed
hating. The gym he'd belonged to these last twelve years a strip
mall's converted K-mart. Rows of treadmills and bikes and
ellipticals. On the walls, a dozen muted flatscreens. Speakers
tucked among the ceiling's girders, the trebly whine of Auto-
Tune. Jason's silent earbuds a guard against socializing and
small talk.

He grabbed the bar, an exhale for his first rep. During
Sophie's illness, this gym was his refuge. The pact he and Alice
had made to spell each other once a day. A break from their
obsessions and vigils. The chance to clear their heads if not
their hearts. Alice with her long walks. Jason here. The sets he
hustled through. The miles he logged on stationary bikes. His
mind allowed to bleed back to the physical. The black-and-
white simplicity of being able to take another step or grind out a
last, quivering rep. He lowered the stack, exhaled, and closed
his eyes.

"Mr. Driscoll?"

The voice came on a tide of lost Saturdays. Rides to the
pool or mall. A voice so entwined with Sophie's he sometimes
struggled to separate one from the other. He opened his eyes.

Beth Wagner stood before him. Little Beth—a secret nickname given by Alice to set her apart from another neighborhood Beth. A soccer teammate. Their duties on student council committees. Little Beth, Sophie's first call when Jason or Alice asked if she wanted to invite a friend. Their sleepless sleepovers, giggles and refrigerator raids. Another sleepover during Sophie's last summer. Beth's head shaved in solidarity, the hair that had started to grow back while Sophie's had not. Rain on the roof, the masking of whispers. Jason's breakfast spread the next morning, sausage, French toast, fresh-squeezed orange juice. Sophie could only nibble, her stomach, the chemo, but Beth was the one who looked sick. At the funeral, Jason embraced her. His shirt damp with her tears. Her tremble in his arms.

Her father beside her. Jason and Stan with their own history. The coffees they shared on chilly sidelines. The night of screams they'd endured at the girls' first boyband concert. Stan had also cried at the funeral. Father and daughter, each with their own kind of sorrow. All of them drowning.

Jason stood. An apology for his smell as he hugged Beth, a handshake for Stan. Stan asked about Alice, and Beth said to send her love. Beth taller than before, her hair different, her braces gone. Jason asked about her first semester at college. The girl's polite answers, her studies and dorm life, and beneath, Sophie's ghost. Their goodbyes as tender as they were awkward. Beth's promise to stop by before she returned to campus.

Jason climbed onto a treadmill. A twinge from the knee that had ended his wrestling career, but while he wasn't as strong as he was then, he knew more about pain. He thought of Beth. A girl. A woman. College. Independence. Love. He turned up the speed then turned it up again. The churn of his legs. The minutes and miles passed. His body's ramping currents. Heart. Lungs. The mechanics that meant nothing and everything. He hit the speed again then a stumble. A fall averted as he grabbed the handrails. His feet straddling a belt that raced beneath him like a black river.

The retirement village's lobby could have passed as a resort hotel's. A grand piano. The staff in matching red polos. Strings of white lights. Poinsettias on every table and counter. Jason sat on one of the red couches and checked the papers in his folder. Attendants pushed two women in wheelchairs. The women side by side, chatting, smiling. On his way in, Jason had passed an ambulance, and he thought of this beautiful room and the polite staff. This last gasp of money's comfort and the truth that didn't care about rich or poor.

The elevator doors opened, and Mr. Keane navigated his walker across the lobby. Jason stood, waved. Mr. Keane's fortune made a quarter at a time in a string of laundromats. His wife dead these past five years. A daughter who visited every other weekend. A son who'd struggled to find himself on fishing boats and oil rigs. Jason guided the old man to the couch and handed him a wrapped box. "A little something for the holidays." In the box, Mr. Kean's favorite bourbon, a gift Jason brought every Christmas.

Mr. Keane waved him off. "If it's what I think, then thanks but no." He patted his stomach. "Doctor's orders."

"Sorry to hear that. I hope the fruit basket will suffice."

"The killjoy will be happy with a fruit basket, but as far as I go, you don't have to do that either."

Mr. Keane different today. Usually they talked before business. The weather. The Eagles. The folly of politicians. But today he was quiet. The fog of eyes and thought. His hand trembled as he initialed and signed. He asked no questions, barely smiled at Jason's attempts at humor.

Jason closed the file. "Is there anything I can do for you, Mr. Keane? Any follow up I can look into?"

He stood, the handles of his walker clenched. A pained straightening. "My children. My daughter I don't worry about, but my son. When the time comes, will you make sure he understands what's been left to him?"

A handshake. The old man's weak grip. "Yes, sir. I will."

* * *

The drive back, and on the way, a new billboard. The little girl, her face backed by the afternoon's clouds. The light turned red, and the girl looked upon him. He'd been braced to find her that day in the woods, each leafy sweep bringing dread then relief then dread again. Weeks had passed, and while she remained missing, she was not yet released from this world, and she lingered among them in hope if not in logic, in that slim, soul-wrapping border some filled with Jesus and men like his father filled with booze.

The car behind him beeped, the light green. He drove on. He'd allotted most of the afternoon to Mr. Keane, and adrift, Jason allowed his body to dictate his route. A journey of reflex. Flannigan's red neon. His old neighborhood. Narrow streets and narrower alleys. Broken windows and corner hustles. The crush of too many people and too little money.

He passed the house where he grew up. After Bill married his mother, they moved away, but this was the home Jason still dreamed about. Its brown tap water. The frost on his bedroom window. His father's voice in cramped rooms. The nights the police came. The nights he fled, sleeping in garages, unlocked cars.

Two blocks away, he parked outside St. Mark's. Its brownstone spire, and on its wide steps, an old woman. A black coat and chapel veil. Her hand on the railing, and each step a struggle. Jason parked just outside the space reserved for hearses and limousines. The steps taken two at a time until he was at her side. "Can I help?" He spoke softly, not wanting to startle her. Her coat's frayed cuffs. Green eyes behind her veil's mesh. A nod, as if she'd been expecting him. She took his arm. A pause atop each step, a breath then up again. He lifted his gaze. The

55

spire lost to the clouds. This homecoming. His grandmother and all the times he'd helped her up these steps. A reunion with this place of faith. His childhood's belief. The adult who'd regressed to magical thinking. The man he was today and the emptiness that was his to fill.

Inside, and the old woman's grip remained tight. His steps timed with hers, and their shoes shuffled over the vestibule's tile, the nave's carpeted aisle. A man slept in a back pew, newspaper stuffed in his boots. Thirty years had passed, yet Jason remembered so much. The must. The lingering incense. The icons. The statue of Mary, flowers around her feet. The old woman stopped, a genuflect, and his hand remained by her back until she slipped into a pew.

Abandoned, Jason considered the statue above the altar. A crucified Christ as large as three men. The statue's weight upon his shoulders as he lowered himself, his hand tapping—Father, Son, Holy Spirit—and slid into the pew across the aisle. The old woman knelt. A rosary in her clasped hands. To Jason's left, Adam and Eve in stained glass, their exile from the garden. To his right, Saint Mark, a gray beard, a lion by his side and a rope by his feet. His bloody martyrdom. His body dragged through the streets. The cruelty of this world and the reward of the next. The sun broke through the clouds. The glass lit, the rise of dust motes—and in that candy-colored instant, a swell in Jason's lungs, a revelation, a sign worthy of Saint Mark and all of this world's mystics and madmen. The truth that if saints were made in God's image, so were sinners. Even killers were His children, especially the ones who didn't have murder in their hearts. And while Saint Mark had been judged by man, there was another judgement that waited, one that mattered so much more.

The old woman hobbled to the confessional, and Jason understood what he needed to do. A confession not to a detective or judge or anyone else in this broken landscape, but to God. He slumped onto the kneeler. His lips grazed his clasped hands. He'd confess to remove the stain that might keep him from Sophie. He'd confess in the hopes that this life's pain and mistakes were just drops in eternity's endless sea.

His tears a surprise, an ambush. A breaking from a place beyond words. Reunion—here was his lifeline. His salvation. He could see her again if his soul was clean. The confession booth door opened. The old woman exited, a kiss for her rosary.

He stood, then the buzz from his pocket. On his phone, a text from Alice. *Come home asap.*

He sped through the afternoon traffic. Blurring roadsides and a singular focus. He squinted. Winter's low sun, the windshield's grit. A hundred thoughts at once. Fingerprints. Cell phone data. Doorbell cameras. A polygraph. The breadcrumbs that linked him to a dead man.

Home, only Alice's car wasn't in the driveway. The mail in the box, the front door left open as he ran upstairs. He knelt in the closet, fumbling, groping. The gun case retrieved. His vague thoughts—Mexico, Canada. A lonely roadside and a bullet through his head.

The front door opened. "Jason?"

The clomp of shoes, the foyer, the stairwell. Alice stopped at the bedroom's threshold. A newspaper in one hand, the other braced against the doorway. He hid the gun and stood. Her embrace rocked him onto his heels, and in his ear, the newspaper's crumple. She stepped back, catching her breath, and handed him the paper. "Here." Her finger jabbed the headline **City Police Discover Link to Suburban Murder.**

Jason read. An apartment searched after neighbors complained of a horrible stench. The tenant bloated, a needle in his arm. The apartment's scales and powders. A wallet linked to a *recent home invasion in the suburbs.*

"Sylvia says that's Roger's wallet." Sylvia an associate in Alice's office, her husband a city detective.

Jason slumped onto the bed. The newspaper in his hands. "I planted the wallet and his watch outside a bar before I came home. My old neighborhood."

She sat beside him. "You didn't tell me that."

"I promised not to tell you anything."

She rubbed his back. "You don't need to tell or think about it again. The story dies with him." She put her arms around him, her body pressed close. Her breath warm on his cheek. "It's over. It's all over, baby."

* * *

The second Saturday of December. Blue skies and a cutting breeze. Here and there, a tumbling leaf. Their cars parked along the cemetery's winding lane. A walk across a gentle slope. Alice ahead with her parents. Jason with his mother, her hand on his arm. Alice's parents the kind who thrived in their retirement community—pickleball and aquacise and sunset walks. Jason's mother's slow fade these past four years without his stepfather. Jason reminded her to eat her bananas, drink her supplement shakes. Her heart with its plastic valves. The silent rooms of the house she refused to leave.

Alice and her parents reached the stone, then Jason and his mother. Each of them with a white lily, Sophie's favorite. Today the second anniversary of her death. In the distance, a graveside service. A dozen or so in black coats. The preacher's words lost on the wind. Alice crouched, clearing leaves, picking grass along the stone's edge, and before she stood, she kissed her fingers and laid them on the stone.

Alice rested her head on her mother's shoulder, and Jason saw her as a child, a girl whose hardest questions couldn't be answered. Jason's mother crying, and perhaps Sophie's death was her fade's greatest catalyst. The house Sophie loved to explore. Their hours in the kitchen. The girl's desire to hear her grandmother's stories, and sometimes Jason eavesdropped, happy his mother had reached a place where she could remember her past with a forgiving heart. Sophie only knew Bill as her grandfather. His real father purged. Photos removed from the family album. A history erased.

Small talk among the grandparents, smiles through their

60

tears. Memories of this girl they loved. Her spirit. Her curiosity. And when they fell silent and the crows in the distant sycamores stopped their cawing, Jason took the paper from his pocket and unfolded it. The paper's edges lifted on the breeze. Her favorite poem. Last year, he couldn't read beyond the first lines. He cleared this throat and spoke into the wind:

"When, in disgrace with fortune and men's eyes,
  I all alone beweep my outcast state,
  And trouble deaf heaven with my bootless cries,
  And look upon myself and curse my fate,
  Wishing me like to one more rich in hope,
  Featured like him, like him with friends possessed,
  Desiring this man's art and that man's scope,
  With what I most enjoy contented least;
  Yet in these thoughts myself almost despising,
  Haply I think on thee, and then my state,
  (Like to the lark at break of day arising
  From sullen earth) sings hymns at heaven's gate:
  For thy sweet love remembered such wealth brings
  That then I scorn to change my state with kings."

He returned the paper to his pocket. He envisioned next year and the year after and ten years after that. The paper's folds fraying. His blurring vision. One by one, they rested their lilies on her stone and bid their goodbyes. Jason rolled the lily's stem between his fingers. Last year, he'd stood here, brimming with grief, lost. Now he wished he could find that place again because the only thing he felt this morning was empty. His shadow over her name, a set of dates. He let the flower drop from his fingers, and he fell with it. A plummet divorced from his body, and even the ground couldn't catch him and he fell and fell and fell.

His mother clutched his arm. "Come on, son. Let's go."

He stepped into the cold and shut the patio door behind him. Evening's early dark, the day's graveside breeze no stronger yet colder. A bite through the slacks and sports coat he'd yet to take off. They'd gone to a restaurant after the cemetery, and there, they skated the thin ice of remembering Sophie without tears, catching themselves with silences and slurps from their water glasses. Alice's parents bid goodbye in the parking lot, a final round of hugs, the promise to make plans for Christmas. Jason and Alice dropped off his mother, and when they returned home, Alice wanted to fuck. "Maybe later," he said, and she hugged him, saying she understood. She changed into her sweats, popped a Xanax, and, within an hour, was asleep on the couch. He pulled the afghan over her, kissed her forehead. The firelight upon her face. He hoped she found the peace in her dreams that he could not. His hauntings of Roger and Sophie. His father's voice from an exhaled cloud. *Shitbird.*

Jason stepped from the patio door's spill of light. The yard dark, and soon the snow, Sophie's grave lost beneath the white months. He turned his back to the breeze and triggered the long lighter he used to spark the fireplace. The flame quivered, shadows on the letter he'd retrieved from the toolbox. He held the flame to the paper's edge. He wasn't just burning the letter. He was burning a life that could have been his, and as the flame caught, he thought of a dead man who'd taken the blame for his crime. The two of them strangers, yet their fates overlapped, and here Jason stood. Alive. Free. Absolved.

He extended his arm. The paper held until the flame singed his fingers. He let go. The paper rose, lifted by its own consumption, this upside-down life. The flame dwindled to ash and faded into the night.

They'd talked about going to the restaurant for over a year. Their friends' raves, the writeups in the local papers. The kind of place where one didn't look at the menu's prices. A piano player at the bar. The waitstaff kept their wine glasses full. Laughter from an adjacent room, a wedding's rehearsal party, toasts and raised glasses. Jason smiled at Alice. She looked pretty, the low light, the sparkle on her earrings. They sat facing each other, and in him, the burden of conversation when they couldn't discuss the things they thought about most.

He twisted the wine glass' stem. A man and woman from the wedding party migrated to the bar. Others joined them, then a pair Jason assumed to be the night's special couple. Shots were ordered, glasses raised, and after they were thrown back, one of the ushers serenaded them all with an a cappella rendition of "Close to You." Applause greeted the song's end, the tables in the restaurant joining in, silverware clinking glasses until the groom and bride-to-be kissed.

Jason thought of his own wedding. The plans he and Alice had made—travel, careers—but ever since they said, "I do," their horizons, once so vast, started to shrink. Dreams delayed then forgotten. The jobs they locked into. Their house beautiful, its *lines of sight*, but also an anchor, and every item they lugged across the threshold only added to its weight. With Sophie, their lives opened up again, but in a way Jason hadn't expected. This world reborn through a new pair of eyes. Then Alice's miscarriages, and with them, another narrowing. The family they'd envisioned replaced by the family they had, and they were rewarded with a child thoughtful and kind, their only heartaches the ones to be expected—first crushes and mean girls, the death of pets and then her grandfather. Then her fatigue, her stomach issues, and Jason would never forgive himself for his initial doubts, for his offered opinions to just get a little more sleep or take it easy on the junk food. A daisy chain of doctors and tests led to her diagnosis, and with it, another narrowing, a hunkering into a single focus. The hope that became their creed. Their private confessions and the salvation they offered each other. Their fears. The pain that pulsed through their home like a dark current and their wish to take it on as their own. Then Sophie's death, and with it, a final constriction, and he thought of the stained glass in Saint Mark's. He and Alice as Adam and Eve, exiles from the garden, naked beneath a deaf heaven.

Alice's finger ran along the glass' rim. "I feel like we should be happy."

"Happy?"

"Relieved then."

He thought of the gun, the things he was braced to do. "Relieved, yes. But I don't know what comes after that."

She studied him.

"What?" he asked.

"Are you happy? Like ever happy?"

He thought for a moment. "No. There are moments I forget. When we're together. I'm happy then, but that fades." He ran a finger over the back of her hand. "When Sophie was sick, you were my rock. Mine and hers. I can't imagine anyone being better than you were then."

She turned up her palm and took his hand in hers. "I think the same about you."

He sighed. They had a chance after Sophie—despite their heartache—to be their best selves. They'd been honorable and good. They'd shouldered their burdens with dignity, but once Sophie left, they grew weak. Their sorrow. Their debt, the circling vultures, and in the crush, they allowed themselves to believe they were owed, a vein of thought that led them to view Roger not as a thief but a balancer of scales. They invited him into their lives and, in the process, lost themselves.

The wedding party donned their coats. Their bright voices. Plans made, the night young and so much ahead.

She withdrew her hand and rearranged her napkin on her lap. "What's left for us if we can't be happy?"

"Maybe it would be enough to keep from getting sadder."

"I don't know if I can live like that." She took a sip of wine and set her glass back down. "Maybe we should do something. Something good."

The last of the wedding party left, and in their wake, a chill from the opened door. "Penance?" he asked.

"Maybe. I don't know."

The waiter set down their plates. The colors and smells, but in Jason, no more joy than when he stood before his office's vending machines. He picked up his fork. "Perhaps you're right."

The drive home. A starless sky. Flurries. The Christmas lights in their neighborhood and the third year their house had gone dark. In their bedroom, another kind of darkness, the same falling sensation he'd felt at Sophie's grave, his only rescue in filling his hands and mouth and allowing Alice the same. Their sex desperate. A consumption, and they clung to each other, their bodies like rafts. This churning sea. This fleeting purification, and when they were done, dazed and catching their breath, he came to, a rising, a melancholy surfacing. The man he was. The things he'd done.

* * *

J ason slowed to keep pace with Madison and her boot. Below them, the midday pit. The glow of screens. The clack of keyboards and staplers. Nathan's chirping banter distinct amid the din, the volume he either couldn't or wouldn't turn down.

Madison's hobble less clumsy than her first day in the boot. "It's pretty straightforward, don't you think?"

"Yes." He stepped ahead and opened the conference room door.

"But the spousal equivalent part seemed a little murky."

He shut the door, the pit's clamor muffled. "I know." But he didn't know, not really. They'd been given the assignment weeks ago, and their agreement was Madison would do the PowerPoint and handouts, and he'd take care of the presentation. "They listen more to you," she'd reasoned. "The good-old-boy network never dies, it just updates its wardrobe and cowers beneath its me-too fears." Truth was he'd barely skimmed the thirty-eight pages of the new Qualified Institutional Buyer statute. The file on his desk, and while he'd managed to highlight a few key points, his eyes had glazed when he attempted any deeper readings.

Madison fired up her laptop while Jason arranged the conference room chairs. "What did you think of the slides?"

"When did you send them?"

"Yesterday afternoon. You didn't—"

"I must have missed it." The avalanche of his inbox. He was drowning in forms and reports, in papers awaiting his signature.

She hooked the laptop to the projector. "I think it's OK.

You know me—I don't cram it with text. Just the main points. Enough to get you rolling."

The little Jason knew was slipping away. Her title slide filled the screen, and she clicked ahead. The slides full of color and clever images, and it was easy to imagine her in high school, the girl who did her homework early then recopied it to hand in something neater. "The one part you'll want to go deeper on are the categories of qualifying persons and identities."

Jason pictured the pages upon his desk. The letters fading beneath the highlighter's yellow. "Do you have notecards?" she asked.

"Listen, Madison, my head's been messed up lately. Things at home. Sophie's anniversary—"

The conference room doors opened. Mr. Smith in the lead. Nathan by his side. The two of them yucking it up. Their rival alma maters. Nathan's Mustang and the vintage Camaro in Smith's garage. The seats filled, the pit's commotion transplanted, the throb in Jason's head as he distributed the handouts. The room with its hierarchies. Mr. Smith in the front row, his arms folded across his chest. Around him, the partners and associates. The pit's hyenas in the rear. Madison turned her back to the others and whispered, "Let's do this together, OK? You start each slide, and I'll fill in when we need it."

Jason welcomed them, a pause until he had their attention. Nathan the last one to turn around, a stick of gum unwrapped and folded into his mouth. Chuckles for Jason's joke about the excitement in store for the next hour. He limped through the first few slides before he started coughing. His throat dry, a scratch he couldn't soothe, the wish he could pause and pour himself a water. The lights suddenly too bright, the room too warm. Sweat on his back. Each heartbeat a tiny panic. His back and forth with Madison stumbled along until he butchered the provisions on qualifying annuities. Madison stepped forward.

The lurch of her boot. The forced smile as she extended her hand and he surrendered the clicker. "To clarify, what Jason means—"

Jason retreated. With each slide, he said a little less. A fading. A dissolving into the shadows. Nathan grinned as he unwrapped another stick of gum.

* * *

J ason, short on money after buying his books for his final
college semester, worked in a restaurant for a few weeks.
He'd landscaped, done construction, but he wasn't
prepared for a kitchen's bustle and cramped quarters. Wasn't
prepared for the barking and fistfights and firings, the amped
currents of short tempers and cheap meth. When he quit, he
vowed he'd take a day with a shovel and a hundred-degree sun
before ever stepping into another kitchen.

Jason thought of that restaurant as he slipped an apron over
his head. Alice did the same, her hair tied back. This kitchen
different than the one he'd worked in, smaller, quieter, cleaner.
The glint of chrome. A spotless floor. Volunteering at the
Hudson Center was Alice's idea. Of course they knew about
the Hudson Center, a building a half mile from the hospital,
and a person driving by could mistake its brick shell for a
daycare or elementary school. Sophie was one of the few locals
in the children's oncology ward. The others from towns sometimes an hour or two away. The Center's mission was to
provide housing for the families of any child who had to stay at
the hospital for an extended period. Some of the Center's units
resembled hotel rooms, others more like apartments complete
with laundry rooms and kitchenettes. Jason and Alice had
known families who'd stayed here—the girl from upstate who
played Minecraft with Sophie as they received their chemo
drips. The mother who kept a flask in her purse. The parents
and children who turned to mist with Sophie's death, and
where, Jason wondered, were they now.

Marge ran the kitchen. Her graying hair tied back in a bun.
A *Kiss the Cook* apron. Steam on her glasses as she stirred a
boiling pot, her instructions to Jason and Alice delivered in a

motherly tone. They'd fill glasses and stock the buffet line. Mainly, they'd offer some cheer to the families and the children who'd been cleared to join their parents for the evening. Around them, the scurryings of two other volunteers. Women just as old as Marge, one thin, the other not, both familiar with the night's routine, both taking a minute to thank Jason and Alice for joining them.

A bell announced dinner. Jason and Alice settled trays into the buffet line, pasta and sauce, roast beef and potatoes. The kitchen doors swung open and shut behind them. Jason felt clumsy beside the two older women, their efficiency, their grace and good humor. The dining area the building's hub, and from it, radiating hallways that brought the night's guests. The thin woman pointed out the boy who'd check in tomorrow morning for his bone marrow transplant. At another table, the teen girls from the in-patient eating disorder clinic, their tiny forkfuls, the nudging and rearranging of their plates' offerings. The girl who shambled forward on crutches and clattering braces, her weeks of physical therapy after her fall from a backyard tree. Jason and Alice behind the serving line. Their cues taken from the others, smiles as they scooped food onto plates.

Christmas music played. *Here comes Santa Claus, right down Santa Claus Lane*, and the night's last arrival emerged from one of the long corridors. A girl of fifteen or sixteen, her mother's hand on her back. The girl bald, pale, translucent. Her body lost beneath a thick sweatshirt. Jason readied her plate, a slice of roast beef, potatoes. "That's enough, thank you," the girl said. A voice like water. Jason asked where they were from, a town he knew, the halfway spot on the ride to Bill's cabin. He and the mother made small talk. The town's restaurants and pizza shops, the statue in its square. He looked over his shoulder, believing Alice had left, but this was not the case.

The others finished, and Jason circulated with a tray of

cookies warm from the oven, and with each offering of the tray, he glanced toward the bald girl. He thought of an art history class he took in college. The Modiglianis. The icons of saints. The girl's handling of her knife and fork deliberate, as if she existed in a denser medium, one that slowed her hands and bent the light that fell upon her. The boy getting the bone marrow transplant asked for another cookie, and the eating disorder girls sang, both sincere and sarcastic, in time with the piped-in music: *It's beginning to look a lot like Christmas.* The girl with the leg braces laughed at her mother's whispered joke. But the room's currents didn't reach the bald girl's table. The girl and her mother silent. The girl's deliberate chewing, and with each swallow, the slightest wince.

Marge circulated, a moment taken to sit at each group. A hand on a shoulder, a smile. An asking of what she could do. When she was done, she stood and made an announcement— there'd be cocoa and an after-dinner showing of *Elf* in the common room. The girl with the crutches thanked Jason and Alice as they bussed her table. One of the eating disorder girls broke a cookie, half handed to her friend, tiny nibbles as they exited. Behind them, the boy performed a sloppy cartwheel before taking his mother's hand. The tables empty save the bald girl and her mother. *Next year all our troubles will be far away.* Marge sat with them. The girl smiled, a polite shaking of her head. Then their retreat, a different hallway than the others. A dwindling into the corridor's shadows.

In the kitchen, Alice loaded the dishwasher while Jason placed the leftovers in Tupperware. The scent of cocoa. The Christmas songs muffled by the shut doors. Alice pale. Brittle.

Marge at the sink, her hands lost in the sudsy water. "Thanks again for coming. We can take it from here." The thin woman poured cocoa into mugs bearing the hospital's logo. Marge lifted the pot from the suds and continued her scrubbing. "There's a sign-up online. I hope you'll join us again." She spoke over the faucet's splash. "This place runs on the kindness of our volunteers."

Jason waited for Alice to say something, but her back was to them as she zipped her coat. "I'm glad we could help," he said. "Thanks for showing us the ropes."

Marge dried her hands and wrapped a stack of cookies in a napkin. "A little treat. There's plenty."

She handed them to Alice. "Thanks," Alice managed.

Outside, a cold drizzle. Haze around the parking lot lights. Alice in front, a stride he couldn't match. He called her, and in her wake, clouds of breath. Halfway across the lot, she threw down the cookies, the broken pieces scattering over the macadam. She reached the car and waited. Her arms hugging her middle, her face turned. Jason hit the fob, and she got in. The door slammed. He started the car, and the dash shone upon her face. They drove in silence. Main Street's Christmas lights glided over the windshield.

"I'm never going back there." She wiped her cheek, her skin glistening. Her jaw set tight. "Never fucking ever."

* * *

Alice set the cookie dish on the coffee table, stepped back, then gave the dish a centering nudge. Last night, she'd retrieved a box of decorations from the attic. Their carved Nativity set. The advent calendar Bill had made in his basement shop, its twenty-five hinged doors. Alice smoothed her skirt, the room taken in. Fingers over her mouth. Judging, perhaps wondering what she'd forgotten. She checked her watch.

"The fireplace. Will you get it?"

Jason crouched by the fireplace. The gas turned on. A squeeze of the long lighter's trigger. A whoosh and a rush of flame. The warmth on his face. Before he could stand, the doorbell rang.

"OK," Alice said. She wasn't speaking to Jason. Her OK a readying of self. A gathering of strength.

Jason stood just beyond the vestibule. Beth framed in the doorway. A new winter coat, the same smile. A hug for Alice. An embrace that lingered, the cold from the opened door. Alice stepped back, Beth's hand in hers, then another hug. Beth's last visit in June. Her senior-week tan. The pictures she'd shared—prom, graduation—and while Jason had smiled and asked questions, he also saw through the images. The shadows beneath. A life unlived.

Beth handed Alice a wrapped loaf, banana and chocolate chip, a gift from her mother. Then a hug for Jason, her chin on his shoulder. "Merry Christmas, Mr. D."

Jason took her coat, commenting on the zipper's ski tags, and Beth told of her father's plans to take them to Stowe before she returned to college. They sat in the living room, Alice and Beth on the couch, Jason in a chair. Alice made tea, and Beth

74

thanked her for the Hershey Kiss cookies, her favorite. Beth kicked off her shoes, her feet tucked beneath her, an inhabiting of old rhythms, and Alice did the same. They talked and Jason listened, buoyed by the warmth of their reunion, by its life, Alice asking to hear it all and Beth obliging. Alice drew near, their shoulders touching as Beth scrolled through her phone's photos. Her dorm. The college's art studio and the canvases from her first painting class. "Who's the cute boy who keeps popping up?" Alice asked.

A blush. "That's Evan."

"And?"

"And I guess we're kind of an item."

Alice brushed Beth's hair behind her ear. A touch she'd offered Sophie a thousand times. "He's a lucky boy."

They drank their tea, and on the plate, more crumbs than cookies. They reminisced, their shared histories—an emergency room visit the day Beth fell off Sophie's skateboard, a rainy day at the beach and the pod of dolphins that leapt just beyond the breakers.

They shared a long laugh, each offering an imitation of a soccer coach whose voice pinched into a squeak when he battled the refs, but in the silence that followed, Jason sensed a divergence, the ever-more-distant paths they'd travel. The futures they couldn't share. They'd be invited to her graduation party, her wedding, but she would fade, taking part of Sophie with her. Beth thanked Alice for the cookies, wished them both Merry Christmas. A pause in the vestibule to zip her coat and a glance up the stairs, perhaps remembering, perhaps still trying to understand. Hugs, well wishes, and when the door shut, Alice lingered at the window, watching as she drove away.

* * *

He woke. The dark window. The wind. A fading dream and the small hours on his clock. He rolled over and realized Alice was awake. Her body motionless. Her eyes opened. "I'm lost," she whispered. "So lost."

Christmas Eve. A nondenominational service in the nursing home's multipurpose room. A plastic tree, its lights reflected on the chrome of walkers and wheelchairs. His mother held her sister's hand. Aunt Connie, always forgetful, now blank. A glimpse of their profiles, and Jason saw them as girls, huddled from thunderstorms, confessing secrets. He rubbed his aunt's shoulder. The feel of bone. By the tree, the staff in their scrubs. Santa hats and reindeer antlers, one with a blinking red nose. Lyrics read off their phones as they sang along with a boombox's CD. *O come let us adore him.* Their voices raised, as if volume might cut through the room's fog.

His mother quiet on the ride home. They passed churches, their lots full, lit stained glass. Then: "Thank you for taking me."

"Glad we could see her."

"I wonder who it's for—me or her."

"Does it matter?"

"Maybe not." He turned onto her street. "It scares me. The thought of ending up like her."

He didn't know what to say. The workings of the mind frightened him as well. He parked and walked her to the door. A final asking if she'd change her mind and stay at his place for the night. A hug goodnight and the promise to call tomorrow.

The ride home, but then not. His route unraveling. Churches. Manger scenes. He thought he'd have no trouble finding Roger's house, but he was wrong. The development's winding streets. The disorientation of Christmas lights. He could have circled back, checked for numbers, but he decided no. He didn't think about Roger less, just differently. The deed existed, unalterable and true, yet the frame he'd constructed had evolved. He'd gone to Roger's to talk him down. To help him—to help them all. He hadn't ripped the wrench from his hand and returned the blow that had left him weak-kneed. He only wanted to wrap his arms around him and bring him to his senses. The tangle of their feet a mistake. He said the words aloud: "A mistake." The phrase repeated as he exited the development and drove home.

He sat in his parked car and studied his house's windows and pictured his life as a series of rooms. Ones he passed through. Ones where he toiled and loved. Ones he'd sealed shut, locks functional yet imperfect, and as he passed, the voices he couldn't stop hearing.

He slid off his shoes in the vestibule. "Alice?"

The house quiet. A stripping back to its heartbeat. The furnace. The refrigerator's hum. He called her again, and when she didn't answer, he guessed she was asleep. He worried about her. Her distance. The pills she'd grown fond of. On the coffee table, a small stack of wrapped gifts. Later, he'd wrap the things he'd bought and set them beside hers, and come morning, they'd open them then try to speed the hours, their greatest wish to put the day and all its memories behind them.

The twinge in his knee as he climbed the steps. The scar that had healed and the tenderness beneath. The upstairs dark save the light that spilled from the bathroom. A peek into their room. The bed empty, and it was then he noticed Sophie's open door.

He paused at the threshold. The curtains pulled back and a starless sky. Alice sat on the bed, her back to him. Her robe, her hair wet. The quilt Alice's mother had sewn from Sophie's baby clothes. The room's heat off. Her bureau's open jewelry box. A dried starfish. Her posters still on the wall, and between them, pages from her sketchbook, still lifes, a self-portrait, bald and smiling.

Alice spoke without turning. "She'd be home right now. Christmas break."

He sat beside her. The mattress sagged. Alice tilted her head and ran a brush through her hair. Dreamy strokes, her eyes on the window. "We'd be having talks about classes and boys and parties." Her brushing slowed. "Sometimes I think about that life, the one I imagined for her. And it feels so real that I swear it must exist."

He put his arm around her shoulder. "She would have gone on to do good things."

He kissed her forehead. She rested her head against his chest, and with her touch, a deep desire. He needed her. Needed her not to be swallowed by the dark. Needed her to breathe. They kissed, and he opened her robe. He was lost. This sea of death, the crack of bone that waited beneath everything he touched, the lifeline of his wife's pulse.

"No," she whispered. "Not here. Not like this."

He picked up her leg, her thigh still warm from the shower. Her robe fell away. Her skin like snow, like moonshine. Her hands on his chest, pushing. "No," she said, but her voice was distant, a surrender. He fumbled, his belt, his zipper. She didn't fight. She only said *no, no*, helpless, frozen. In his thoughts, the certainty he'd die without her. The knowing death was with them, in this room, in their blood. She turned her face until he was done. Both of them crying.

II

* * *

Madison visited Jason's office after her quarterly review. Their private jokes. The boss's monogrammed cufflinks, his habit of blinking every time he mentioned the partner who'd died less than a month after being strongarmed into retirement. "It's like something out of Poe," Madison said. "Like he keeps hearing the beating of his hideous heart."

Jason smiled. This mask and the truth beneath. The heartbeats he alone heard. Alice's silences. The way she now shrank from his touch and their bed unshared. Madison with her own pain, and in him, the sudden urge to embrace her. To comfort her. The desire to look into a pair of eyes and not see the reflection of a monster.

Madison pointed to the papers on his desk. "What's this?"

"I accidently printed two copies of a report."

She shook her head. "You know how the boss feels about waste." She took a sheet and crumpled it into a ball. "Paper. Toner. Ink. At least you didn't use any staples." She raised her hands, the shooter's form from her high school basketball days. A high arc and the paper rattled into the waste can.

Jason balled up a paper, but his shot bounced off the can's rim. "So how was your review?"

"I had a good quarter. Which means I'll have to have a better one come spring. Then a better one after that." Another shot, her aim true, her follow-through held for a moment. "We're not supposed to catch the rabbit, you know. We're only supposed to run until we drop. Hopefully at the end we'll have a few healthy years and enough cash to never think of that fucking rabbit ever again."

"I used to like it here." Another crumpled paper, another miss. "I used to be more like Nathan than I care to admit."

83

"Nathan?"

"Zimmy."

"Oh." She smiled. "I can see that."

"I hope I was less obnoxious. But I was competitive. Everyone had a score. There were winners and losers. But now," he looked away from his desk's framed picture, "now I do it not to be poor. Do it because I don't know who I am without it."

She picked up the blue stress-ball stamped with the logo of their new insurance provider. "You could walk out of here and get a job before the weekend."

"Just another parallel universe. Nothing important would change."

She tossed the ball and snagged it with her opposite hand. "And what universe do you want to land in?"

He thought for a moment. "I don't know."

His phone rang. The boss's secretary. Jason hung up, put on his suitcoat. "This isn't going to be pretty."

She stood, a bit lopsided, the boot's skewed alignment. She brushed lint from his shoulder. "Whatever universe you end up in, there's going to be a new boss."

"Same as the old boss?"

She patted his shoulder. "Same as the old boss."

His walk above the pit. A rattle from Nathan's desk, a shaker bottle, his post-workout powders. The boss's secretary buzzed him in, a flashback to Jason's childhood. A visit to the principal. A one-sided conversation. The imparting of hard truths. The fact that Jason was treading water while others soared. The fact that business was business.

Mr. Smith behind his desk. This room of glare and reflections. His hands folded atop the desk's blotter. "I know these past two years have been hard."

"Yes, sir,"

Smith went on, offering hope yet careful to lay out the implications of not hitting his numbers. Outside, the cold sun, and his boss's voice faded into the building's undertones. Jason knew his reprieve was rooted in pity—and true, he hated Nathan, but at least he was spared his pity—and as his boss droned on about *opportunity* and *obstacles* and *rebounding,* Jason's fists clenched. The anger that his daughter's death had become a currency, even though that currency was the only thing keeping him afloat.

Smith closed Jason's file and took off his glasses, a gesture of concern. "Let's hope for better things moving forward, shall we, son?"

J ason paused on the front porch. His belly knotted, his eyes dry. The extra hours he'd put in after the others had left. His day choked with paperwork and calls and emails. A screen's glare and the rattle of his wheel. The door double-locked, and he fumbled with the key.

The threshold, and the cold mingled with the scent of smoke. Alice sat at the kitchen table. This house of open spaces. She exhaled and ground her cigarette into an ash-littered butter dish. The only light came from the kitchen, and just above her head, a hazy strata. She'd been crying, her eyes and face red, but she wasn't crying now. She shook another cigarette from her pack. "Warm up dinner if you want. It's in the fridge."

He walked past her, and the smoke stirred. He didn't know what to say, so he said nothing. On the table, the day's mail. Bills. Another flyer for the missing girl, a coat of purple and pink. He made a plate, stuffed shells, sausage. His stomach, so delicate these days, would revolt later. The microwave hummed. The plate's slow turn. On the wall, Sophie's penciled rendition of their house. Three windows, three faces. The paper's white fading. He carried the plate to the table. She sucked a deep drag and exhaled. She didn't bother to look at him.

He'd failed to kneel before God, that day he almost confessed, but he knelt now, his head on her lap. The words he wanted to say, his wooden tongue. The fear all he could offer her was darkness. The fear he'd never stop falling. He needed her touch. He needed her fingers in his hair. A stroke of his cheek. Needed to be assured he was still worthy of being loved.

He waited. Breathing her in. His cheek on her thigh. He felt her currents, the cigarette brought to her mouth, the in-and-out of her lungs. He waited, his thoughts a spiral of prayers and silent bargains. Just a touch. One touch.

The room iced over, and when she stubbed out her cigarette and lit another, he returned to his seat. The scrape of his fork. Silence and her eyes upon him as he ate.

* * *

The morning's cold faded inside the hotel lobby. An open space, and five stories up, skylights, and above them, a river of gray clouds. The space's muddled acoustics, voices that rose and dissolved. Behind Jason and Alice, the silent hour-and-a-half ride to Baltimore. Farms and industrial parks. The beltway. The Inner Harbor's glass towers. Her company's annual retreat. The lobby wide, and along its perimeter, restaurants, a bar. A series of conference rooms, each marked by a placard that bore her company's blue-and-white logo. The Susquehanna Room. The Chesapeake Room. The Charles Room. In one, the waitstaff arranged a snack table. In the next, IT workers fiddled with wires and projectors.

Someone called Alice's name, and Jason followed her to a check-in table. Around the table, balloons of blue and white. Placards listed the day's events. Breakout rooms. Headshots of motivational speakers. Alice signed in and selected her name from a spread of pre-printed tags. Jason studied the tags and thought of one unprinted. And he thought of the push of life and commerce and how Roger's name would only be mentioned in passing, a flicker before it drowned in the lobby's sea of voices.

Alice smoothed the tag onto her blazer. "Check in's not until 2:00."

"I'll entertain myself until then." He leaned forward. She stiffened as his lips grazed her cheek.

Someone called her name, and Alice didn't offer a goodbye before leaving to help a coworker. Jason unclaimed by the lobby's bustle. No tag waited with his name, no one stepped forward to shake his hand, and he found the detachment both lonely and pleasant. Faces glided by, like his but strangers. The lobby's glass elevator descended, and in it, a child, his hands pressed to the glass. An expression of wonder.

The hotel on the harbor, and he walked out. The breeze stronger here, and on the water, ripples and crests, the bay's open scent. Gulls hovered, landed, then scattered as he neared. Paddle boats locked up for winter clunked with the water's rise and fall. The harbor's edge marked by a wide, brick promenade, a lineup of shops and restaurants. The science center at one end, and at the other, the aquarium. On the promenade, bundled couples, most with children in tow. A group of young girls passed. The girls paired off. Their chaperones' urgings for all to keep up. The girls passed Jason, and at the line's end, two stragglers, their hands held as they hurried to rejoin the others. A gust blew the purple cap from one of the girl's heads. Jason picked up the cap and called: "Hey! Hey, little girl!" The line halted, and the chaperones turned as Jason jogged over and returned the cap. The girl's "Thank you" barely a scratch against the breeze.

He sat on a bench. The water bled into a misted horizon. He shivered, clutched his collar. He thought about the empty hours until he could check in. The line of little girls at the promenade's far end, and he stood and followed them into the aquarium.

He'd been here years ago. Sophie and Beth barely older than the girl in the purple cap. Another life. Inside, and he remembered the workers' blue shirts. Remembered the piped-in whale songs. Remembered the sharks' glide. The rays' dreamy flaps. He rode the escalator, and beside it, a whale's skeleton, and through its bones, a glimpse of the purple cap. A giant tank rose three stories through the building's heart, and he walked the curved ramp outside its glass. Around him, the day's tourists, his footsteps part of a greater harmony, the movements of people and fish. Blue light spilled over him and the children who hurried by, their bodies sometimes brushing his coat, their excitement. Echoes all around. The ramp circled up, and in the tank, another circling, a shark, sleek and long. Eyes blacker than night. Behind it, three more sharks. Jason mesmerized by the sharks' sway and rhythm. These evolutionary wonders. These beasts. Their life of motion and reflex, of survival, and in Jason's mind, the sharks' prowl churned itself into words *I did what I had to do I did what I had to do I did what I had to do.*

Outside, he bought a lamb kabob from a vendor and returned to his bench. Gray sky. Gray water. This life he knew and the mystery beneath. He ate and felt better for it. He returned to the hotel. The lobby quieter, the conference room doors shut. He checked in. The glass elevator lifted, and below, a little girl turned from her mother, watching. Their room on the fourth floor, and after locking the door, Jason paused by the window. Fog crept over the harbor. Children raced along the promenade, and in him, the desire to warn them, the danger so close. He drew the curtain, stretched out on the bed, and fell asleep.

* * *

That evening, Jason and Alice returned to their room. They'd eaten dinner in the banquet hall. A speech from the CEO. The importance of vision, of standards and ethics. A standing ovation for a new incentive program. A table with Alice's officemates. Faces he knew, names he struggled to remember, the day's tags shed. Small talk and prime rib, drinks and loosened tongues. Burt from HR told a joke, and when the table erupted, Jason thought of the aquarium's circling sharks. Their lack of memory, their ever-forward glide.

Jason sat on the bed and watched Alice slip out of her dress. At dinner, she'd included him in her conversations, and he played the part of the happy husband. Here, she returned to making him invisible. Her silences, her distance. A mirror above the dresser, and she studied herself as she removed her jewelry. Jason's reflection eclipsed when Alice reached for her buzzing phone. She tapped out a text then another.

"Who is it?"

"A friend." She sent another message. "Arlene. She works in the Arlington office. She wants us to meet her for drinks in the bar."

Jason turned on the TV. His thumb on the remote, a parade of images. He didn't feel like drinking. Didn't feel like playing the happy husband. "Been a long day," he said.

"It has." Alice leaned close to the mirror, her finger tracing her cheek. "She's nice though. And I told her we would. Just for one."

She changed into her jeans, a white blouse. He took off his tie and suitcoat. She grabbed her purse and stood in front of the TV. "I'm going. You can come if you'd like."

They rode the glass elevator to the lobby, a slow descent.

The doors opened, and he looked up. The skylights dark, the press of fog.

The bar near the entrance. A muscled doorman. A dim hallway. The bar lit, but only barely, and Jason paused, waiting for his eyes to adjust. A dance song thumped. The bar with a few empty seats. A waitress passed, drinks balanced atop a hoisted tray. Along the wall, black-vinyl booths where candles in hurricane glasses burned atop glass tables. Jason disoriented by the glitter of mirrors and chrome. Laughter from the booths, shadowed faces. Ahead a small dancefloor, pivoting lights of orange and red. On the floor, three young women. None of them enthusiastic, their drinks in-hand. Their sway tuned to a rhythm duller than the speakers' thump.

A woman rose from a booth, a wave, a shout: "Alice!" The women hugged. Jason leaned forward, straining to hear the introductions. Arlene, short and curvy, a smile that plumped her cheeks. Her husband Dan the lanky kind. Sharp creases in his khakis and an untucked black shirt. A face that had seen a lot of sun. They shook, his hand callused the way Jason's had been the college summers he worked construction. Alice and Arlene occupied the same roles in their offices, their past ten months of emailing and video conferencing. Arlene's joke that they were work-twins, sisters from different misters. They slid into the booth, Arlene and Alice in the middle, Jason and Dan on the ends.

Dan waved down the waitress, insisting the first round was on them. Arlene clutched Alice's arm and doubled over laughing, and Jason remembered looking in his rearview, how Sophie and Beth carried on in the backseat. Dan, he inferred, worked for the government, a contractor of some sort, the details unshared. The music loud, and after a fitful, shouted exchange, Dan and Jason abandoned their attempts at small talk. Dan sat back, raised his glass, and Jason did the same. An acknowledgement that the evening was about their wives, who hadn't stopped chatting and laughing. Arlene's hair so black it bled into the bar's dark. Her silver necklace and matching bracelet. Her blouse's open top and the squeeze of cleavage.

Jason's straw pushed his ice cubes. Two men strayed onto the dancefloor. An attempt to join the women, but the women turned their backs, the men sentenced to continue their sad gyrations until the song ended. Jason thought of the old man who'd slapped him in Flannigan's and pictured him slapping him again for drinking in a place like this. Then Jason imagined Flannigan's and here as not so different in the most important ways. Their murky waters. Their masks and desperations. He wondered if he and Alice would leave after their drinks or if they were obliged to return the favor and buy the next round.

Yet he also found himself smiling, not having fun so much as being entertained by Arlene. Her stabs of laughter. The way she brushed back her hair, exposing the ear she brought to Alice's lips. The dancefloor's rotating lights splashed over them, and in the shine, the wetness of her eyes, her jewelry's silver glint. And when Arlene laughed, so did Alice, and the sight filled his heart then broke it. The smile he'd missed. The fear he'd never make her happy again.

The waitress returned, and Jason did buy the next round, and when their drinks arrived, Dan offered a toast to new friends. The tune the DJ had been playing wound down, and the rejected men abandoned the dancefloor, the women too, and the spinning lights illuminated the empty space as the DJ spoke over the next song's intro. "It's time to take you all back, folks. Let's see who remembers this one."

Arlene sipped her drink. "I think this motherfucker's implying I'm old."

Dan said something that made her laugh, and she kissed his cheek. Alice bobbed her head. Long ago, they'd danced to this song, her college house, a kitchen floor sticky with spilled beer. Arlene rested her head against Alice's, and together, they sang the first chorus. Jason thought of the twins joke, the irony of their differences, blond hair and black, tall and thin, short and round, yet in this light, both of them beautiful.

Dan rested his elbows on the table, his voice raised. "You like this song, Alice?"

"It takes me back."

"Want to dance?" He turned to Jason. "That OK?"

Alice turned to him. "Unless you'd rather."

Jason stood. Alice slid over, and Dan extended a hand, a gentleman's gesture. Jason returned to the booth. Alice's first steps rusty, the years that had passed since their last dance. He thought of the semester he blew out his knee, the clunky brace and how watching her dance with her girlfriends filled him with a desire both painful and sweet.

Arlene said something he didn't catch, and when Jason scooched closer, Arlene did the same, their hips touching before she settled back. "I'm glad you guys could join us."

"Me, too. Thanks."

"It's nice to shake off a day of corporate bullshit."

"I know." Alice looser now, the athleticism of a girl who grew up in the Title IX generation. "Dan's a good dancer," he said.

"He is." She lifted her drink. "Me, I have two left feet."

"I'm not the best either."

Her lips on her straw, a smile. "I'll bet you have a few slick moves."

"Perhaps back when. Or at least I may have thought so after a few beers."

"In a galaxy far, far away."

"Very far. Very far indeed."

A new song started, and Arlene nodded toward the dancefloor. "Look at her. She's been a godsend, she really has. She's helped me out a lot." Another sip. "Looks like she's enjoying herself."

It did look like she was enjoying herself. Her arms raised as she and Dan resurrected The Bump. "It's good to remember the old days," Arlene said. The buttons on her blouse strained as she rearranged herself, her elbows on the table and her fist on her chin. "It's good to be reminded of that time when the world was full of possibilities."

"Are you saying you have access to a time machine?" He stabbed his straw into his drink. "Because I, for one, would be very interested."

"I'll bet you're secretly pretty good at it."

Jason leaned forward. "Excuse me?"

She scooted closer. The smell of her. The push of her breast against his arm. "Dancing. Good at dancing." Her hand rested on his thigh. "Among other things."

He looked down. The glass tabletop. Her hand below, a squeeze. He didn't move. On the dancefloor, Dan and Alice shimmied in a loose synchronicity. Jason's finger wagged from Arlene to her husband, and he surfaced into a new understanding. "Wait. This is what you're proposing? You and him?"

Arlene removed her hand and lifted her drink. Another smile around her straw before she sipped. "Proposing? More like imagining. Don't you ever imagine, Jason?"

A new song, and Alice and Dan left the dancefloor. Alice's cheeks flushed. She sat, held her glass to her forehead. "That was a workout."

Arlene slid to the booth's other side and stood to join her husband. "I think Dan and I will go to the bar for a shot." She lifted herself onto her tiptoes and kissed his cheek. "We'll be back in a few."

After they left, Jason turned to Alice. "He wants to fuck you."

She pulled back from the drink she'd brought to her mouth. "We were just dancing. Don't get weird."

"No. He does." Jason leaned closer. "She told me. And she wants to fuck me."

Alice opened her mouth, but before she could speak, Arlene and Dan returned, each carrying two shot glasses. Arlene offered a glass to Alice, Dan to Jason. Arlene raised her voice against the music. "We've had a great time, but I think we're going to retire." She lifted her glass and Dan did the same, and after a pause, so did Alice and Jason. "To a fun night," Dan said. Then Arlene: "And new friends."

They threw back their shots. The warmth and bite in Jason's throat. Arlene squeezed Alice's hand. "Let's be in touch, OK, sweetie?"

Arlene and Dan left, his arm over her shoulder. Alice rocked her empty shot glass on the tabletop, staring, quiet. Jason finished his drink. "That was fucked up," he said.

Alice shook her head, bit her lip.

"I mean, did you see that coming?"

"No." She shook her head. "Not at all."

Ten minutes later, they rode the glass elevator. The lobby receded. This perspective of dreams. Then their floor. The long hallway, identical doors to the left and right. The slide of a card and a tiny light turned from red to green. Inside, and still they hadn't talked, and Jason thought of his first high-school concussion, the world's warp, the frayed wires between understanding and speech. Alice in the bathroom. The fan on, but her cigarette's smoke threaded into the room.

Jason leaned in the bathroom doorway. Alice in front of the mirror. Her left arm hugging her belly, her right elbow propped on the opposite hand. She stared into her own eyes. The lazy cradle of her cigarette. A wisp of rising smoke.

"It will be weird, seeing her tomorrow," Jason said.

She sucked a drag, and her exhale masked her reflection. She brushed by him and sat on the bed. He waved at the smoke. "Don't want to set off the alarm."

She dropped the cigarette and ground it beneath her shoe.

He sat beside her, picked up the butt, and brushed away the ashes. "Alice?"

She pulled out her phone. The screensaver photo, her and Sophie, cheek to cheek. She looked at the photo and then to him. "Do you want to call or should I?"

In the bathroom, Jason splashed water over his face. He knew where he was, but he was lost. He heard Alice, a one-sided conversation, the giving of their room number. Back in the room, he tried to speak, to plead, but Alice refused to look at him. He paused at the door. She stared into the mirror above the bureau. "Room 224," she said. She undid her blouse's top button and traced her fingers over the base of her throat.

The hallway quiet. Dan stepped off the glass elevator as Jason waited to board. Dan's wide smile, and as they passed, he patted Jason's back. "Enjoy, my brother."

* * *

The next morning, the four of them met outside the breakfast buffet. Dan and Alice already waiting. Arlene, upon seeing them, left Jason's side. A hug for her husband, a greeting common to train stations and airports. The traveler's return. Jason and Dan in last night's rumpled clothes. Far above, the hotel's skylights. Blue skies and sun, all of them paler in the streaming light.

A hostess seated them. The plates they brought to the buffet still warm from the dishwasher. Trays of sausage and bacon. French toast. Cantaloupe and melon. Dan in the lead, his heaping plate. Arlene's joke that he *must've worked up some appetite.* Jason at the end. He snuck glances at Alice. Last night, he'd felt invisible. This morning, he was erased.

They settled in. Arlene's jokes. Her plate nearly as full as her husband's, an echo of how she'd been in bed. Needy. Hungry. The fullness of her hips and breasts. The weight she brought down upon him. Her eagerness to provide a dirty narration. A family at the next table held hands and bowed their heads, and Jason remembered it was Sunday.

Dan and Arlene carried the bulk of the conversation, and Jason felt himself fading, the moment knowable but everything beneath slippery, who belonged to whom and what was right and what might snuff his soul's last speck of goodness. He nodded, forced an occasional smile, but said little. Alice stood, but when she asked if anyone wanted anything, she didn't look at Jason. Arlene asked if Dan would fetch her more coffee. He kissed her temple. "Yes, my queen."

When they were alone, Arlene laid her hand atop Jason's. A different touch than the hand that had inched up his thigh in a dim bar booth. This touch empathetic, almost motherly. "It's

98

OK to feel awkward the next morning. It's all so new." She smiled, looked back to the brunch line, and removed her hand. "I had a great time. I had a feeling you'd be a good one when I saw you. I just didn't know how good." Alice returned. Steam from the coffee cup Dan set in front of Arlene. "My lady."

Later, the ride home. The city's skyline in the rearview. The traffic thinning. The highway's construction zones and billboards so ugly he took a random exit, pointed them in more or less the right direction, and drove. Alice said nothing, and they took in the rolling hills. Pastures with grazing horses. Valley towns colored in soot and rust. He tuned in a radio station from their town, and the voices came and went amid the static.

He didn't know what they could say to each other beyond the things that would hurt the most. They crested a ridge. A trash fire's smoke rose from a field. The ashy ribbon rising, thinning, this bright morning. The radio signal clearer here, and when Alice heard the news, she turned up the volume. The little girl found. Alive. Shivering in her purple and pink windbreaker along a barren upstate road.

Alice turned to him. Her eyes brimming. The earth in which they'd buried Sophie had opened and offered a child back to the world. Alice reached for his hand. He pulled onto a weedy shoulder, horses on the other side of an electric fence. They held each other. Crying. Saying nothing.

* * *

Mrs. Forsythe clutched her purse as her son railed. Mrs. Forsythe's snowy hair and faltering hearing aids. Eleven years a widow, and Jason had helped her navigate the selling of her husband's cheap apartment units, their conversations always centering around James, her only child. The portfolio and holdings she wanted him to inherit, her worries about her James and his knack for self-sabotage. The Ivy League college he'd been kicked out of. His failed marriages and business ventures. James ten years older than Jason, but this morning, James Forsythe the third assumed the role of petulant teen as his index finger jabbed the printouts he'd tossed onto Jason's desk. "How could you advise such a thing? How could you not alert her that this was underperforming? If you'd just followed the market's trend, you could have doubled her return these past five years."

He'd dealt with James Forsythe before, his shallow understandings and deep-running ignorance. Jason suppressed the desire to snuff his complaints with a mid-sentence punch to the mouth. Instead, he searched for a calm tone and spoke, "Mr. Forsythe, your mother and I sit down every year and create a plan of action. Many investors of a certain age want to shift their holdings to more secure structures."

James spoke as if his mother wasn't there, and indeed, in the morning light, she appeared to be rendered in watercolors, blurred at the edges, fading before their eyes. "She can't comprehend all those intricacies. It's your job to be her advocate. Her advisor." He crossed his arms over his chest. "I won't have my mother treated this way. I demand to see your supervisor."

Calls were made, and Jason walked the Forsythes to his

boss's office. The pit's chatter. Nathan at the copier, a salute as Jason passed, and Jason wondered if the kid was now openly fucking with him. Jason filled his lungs before entering Mr. Smith's waiting area. He'd documented his meetings with Mrs. Forsythe, her wishes honored, her options thoroughly explained, and five minutes with James would be enough for his boss to understand where the trouble lay. Still, Jason was dumping his problems on Smith's desk, and no matter how right he was, he was the deliverer and—by association—a conspirator in the shit-dumping that would disrupt Smith's cherished morning read of *The Wall Street Journal*.

Mr. Smith greeted Jason and the Forsythes in his waiting area. The old man diplomatic, and after escorting mother and son into his office, he dropped his smile and told Jason to wait for his call. His door shut. A look from his secretary, her stare multiplied in the pit as Jason returned to his office.

He closed his door and paced around his desk. He ground his fist into his opposite hand, punched his chest, once and again. He snatched the nameplate holder from his desk. The holder lifted, a pose of threat, the violence of kinetic energy, of a rage that burned brighter than his notion of self.

A knock. The door's lever twisted. Madison's voice: "Jason?"

"Hey." He set down the nameplate holder and shoved his hands into his suitcoat's pockets.

She closed the door behind her. She wore a gray skirt and a matching blazer. A white blouse open at the throat, a simple gold chain. A white sneaker and her clunky boot. "What's going on?"

They claimed the chairs where the Forsythes had been sitting, the seats turned to face each other. Jason with his elbows on his knees. Madison assured him their boss would see through James's foolishness, then a smile. "But you're right about interrupting his morning paper time."

"It's not that." Jason rubbed his hands over his face, his eyes hidden. "It's not that."

Madison rested a hand on his shoulder. "Are you OK?"

Jason opened his eyes but didn't look at her face. In him, the crossing of wires, the blindness of a hundred shooting sparks. He laid a hand on her knee. A pause before he looked into her eyes.

"Jason—"

He pushed his hand up. The meat of her thigh, its warmth and muscle. Her skirt bunched in her lap.

"Fuck, Jason!" She stood, an escape made awkward by her boot. Her chair tumbled to the floor. "What the fuck are you thinking?"

* * *

Arlene sat up and turned on the nightstand lamp. The wide hotel bed, the sheet over her lap. The sag of her breasts and the mess of her black hair. She looked down upon Jason, the smile of a gentle giant. "Well you were up for it tonight, weren't you?" She took a hit off her vape pen, her chin lifted, a smoky exhale. She held the pen to Jason's mouth. "Some indica. Bring you down from your work week."

An expansion in his lungs. A billowing exhale. Arlene took another hit, her voice pinched as she held the smoke. "It's what the doctor ordered for worried minds." She exhaled. "I can tell you've got a worried mind sometimes, don't you, baby?"

Jason rolled onto his side. His finger traced Arlene's arm, the soft hair, a circling of a mole. Behind him, another Friday. Birthday cake in the breakroom. Madison's refusal to look at him let alone accept his apology. Another kind of silence on the ride to Baltimore. Last night, he and Alice had fucked for the first time since Christmas Eve. Her request surprising him, the hope of being forgiven or at least claimed, but he soon realized the act was purely mechanical. A checking of parts. A shaking off of rust.

He rose, naked, and in the bathroom, filled two glasses with water. He handed one to Arlene. "Thanks, babe."

Babe, her easy smile, the tender way she stroked his chest after they'd used each other—she was full of little intimacies, and Jason was thankful for them, desiring them more than the body she offered. She and Alice had been in touch since the company retreat. Work things mainly, but also hints, the notion of meeting up floated in a general way that grew more specific until they settled on this weekend. When Alice brought up the invitation, Jason said yes, not because he desired Arlene, but because he'd forfeited his right to a higher morality. His only stipulation—they could share their bodies but not their truths. Roger, of course. Jason's derelict father. And most of all, Sophie. Not a word, ever.

He turned off the nightstand light. He felt his way across the room and pulled back the curtains. Below, the harbor lights. The expanse of dark water. Bundled couples hurried beneath the lights and slipped back into the night. He thought of the lobby's bar, its glitter and chrome. Thought of a room identical to this one and what Alice might be doing.

The vape's tip shone in the window as Arlene took another hit. "We're happy this worked out." She exhaled. "We like you guys."

Jason went to close the curtain. "No," she said. "Keep it open." He returned to bed. She held the vape to his lips. His eyes had adjusted, and she looked upon him. "I know what you're thinking."

"Oh yeah?"

"You're thinking 'How did I end up here with this little woman with big tits who wants nothing more from me than what I want from her?'"

He ran his finger around her nipple. "Maybe. Maybe something like that."

She pulled back her hair and tied it in a quick knot. He rubbed her back, the nubs of her spine, the soft roll around her middle. She looked over her shoulder. "I think the world's like that sometimes, beneath all the politeness and such. We all want the things we're afraid to ask for." She reached for his cock, squeezing it beneath the sheet. A smile as he stirred, and she pulled down the sheet and knelt before him. "Sometimes we don't know what we want until it falls into our lap."

* * *

Their brunch the next morning less strained, and in Jason, a new thought, the hope that perhaps he and Alice, through their infidelities and abandonment of tradition, could stake out a new life. Perhaps not a better one, but one they could salvage from the wreckage. One less haunted by ghosts. The things they'd done. Their little girl.

The museum was Dan's idea. An exhibition of abstract painters. "I was an art history minor in college," Dan said, and although Jason had no reason to doubt it, he wondered if this was true. Dan himself struck Jason as an abstraction. His trendy shirts. His necklaces. The tanning-bed brown of his cheeks and his white, white teeth. The job he didn't talk about. "Clearance issues. Sensitive topics," he confided as they waited for their Uber. Jason's reflection in the lenses of his lowered aviator glasses. A wink. "I know how to keep a secret."

The museum uptown. Greek columns flanked the entrance. Inside, galleries named for the city's moneyed families, high ceilings, muffled echoes. The rooms with their lazy rhythms. The gatherings that paused then dispersed. Dan pointed out Klee and de Kooning. Their textures. The chains they broke. Jason understood the chain-breaking thing was directed at him. Dan's nod letting Jason know he was now one of them. The unchained. The free.

They stopped before a canvas longer than the four of them laid head-to-toe. "It's kind of wild, isn't it?" Arlene said. "Dan knows all the technical terms, but this is the kind of thing I can lose myself in, you know?"

Jason considered the profiles of Arlene and his wife. Their gaze upon the canvas, each lost in their own thoughts. He turned back to the painting. The colors swirled, vibrated.

Jason's lack of sleep, his day's drift. The vertigo of this unchained world.

Dan spoke: "Those classes changed me. I came to see how the history of art wasn't just a mannered evolution. It was a series of chances and dares. Of revolution. Leaps into nothing, blind in a way but guided by a new vision. Most failed, of course." Jason startled when Dan clamped his shoulder. "But some soar."

A ding, then another. Arlene dug her phone from her purse. Dan held his phone, too. They exchanged smiles, and Arlene turned to Alice. "There's a party tonight. Friends of ours outside town. You absolutely have to come with us."

* * *

E vening found Jason and Alice in the backseat of Dan's coupe. His gearshift jerks and abrupt lane changes. The lights' ebb and flow. The harbor behind them, and now, crowded neighborhoods glimpsed from the freeway. A panorama of lit windows and other lives. A merge onto the belt-way, and within ten minutes, an exit sign Jason didn't catch, the ramp's corkscrew and his shoulder pressed into Alice's. A few miles, a turn, a few more miles and another turn, and soon, Jason lost what little sense of direction he'd possessed. He sat behind Dan, Arlene lit by the dash. The scent of weed as she passed the vape to Alice. A skid. Black ice, this moonless night. "Easy, cowboy," Arlene said. "We want to make it there in one piece."

Jason uncomfortable. The cramped backseat. Dan's driving. The deeper discomfort of not knowing where they were going, their decision to come questioned more with each mile. Arlene talked about the host, a man named Jake. The house he and his wife had been building for the past year. Arlene had seen the pictures. The house *fabulous*. The parties at their old house in town *fabulous*. *Fabulous*, the word lingered, thick as the vape's skunky cloud. Everything was going to be *fabulous*.

Arlene turned to Dan. "We should bring a gift, shouldn't we? A housewarming."

"You're bringing yourself, aren't you?" Dan leaned over the console, a cheek offered for Arlene to kiss, their joined silhou-ettes. The car drifted across the double-yellow. "What better gift could Jake want?"

They got lost, U-turns on gravel lanes. Arlene texting,

Jake's development so new it wasn't on their phones. A wooded patch, and outside their windows, the tangle of bare trees. "Here! Here!" Arlene said, and as they turned, Jason glimpsed the bob of staked balloons.

The road unmarked, and the fresh macadam glistened in their headlights. The land cleared, and they passed bulldozers and backhoes. Dug foundations. Portable toilets. The road ended in a cul-de-sac lined with cars. Here, a few structures framed out, wooden skeletons. One with a roof. One complete, lights in the windows, a jack-o-lantern shine. A house three times as large as Jason and Alice's.

A yard of mud-frozen tire tracks. Colder here, and Jason thought of his stepfather's cabin, the countryside's chill. Dan tugged Arlene's hand as they wove between the driveway's wedged cars. Arlene turned as Dan lifted the door's brass knocker. A schoolgirl's grin. "Isn't this wild?"

Two muscled men, one black and bald, the other with feathered blond hair, greeted them at the door. Dan and Arlene held up their phones. Dan scrolled to another text and showed it to the black guard. "Jake's cool with our friends coming."

Jason squinted in the foyer. A black curtain at the foyer's other end, and from the curtain's other side, music. The foyer just large enough for the six of them, and Arlene laughed, the bumping of shoulders and elbows as they shed their coats. The blond guard checked Arlene and Alice's purses while the black one opened a velvet cinch bag. Dan and Arlene placed their phones inside, the bag held open until Jason and Alice did the same. Arlene's arms held wide as the blond guard patted her down. She laughed. "Easy there, big fella. I hardly know you." Alice next, her arms outstretched.

One of the guards pulled the curtain aside, and before passing, Dan took a mask from a bowl. He secured it over his eyes. The look of a movie thief. His eyes' white crescents, a field of black. He turned to Jason. "In case you want to get your Lone Ranger on."

Jason took a mask but didn't put it on. The threshold curtain brushed his neck, and on the other side, he paused. Here was a home rich in lines of sight, the openness accentuated by the sparse furnishings. A blue bulb in one lamp, red in another. In the floor's center, a gathering at a portable bar. A bartender, a pressed white shirt and black bow tie. A topless woman passed, glitter on her breasts, a martini in each hand. To Jason's right, a long couch, its back to them. A few sitting, others standing. None talking, all with gazes fixed, and before Jason reached the bar, he spotted the trio of writhing bodies on the living room rug. An open stairwell behind the bar, a couple going up and a woman coming down, the three of them stopping on the middle's landing to kiss.

At the bar, Arlene donned her mask, and Alice did the same. Jazz played, a bluesy horn. The topless woman handed one of her drinks to a bald man then rested her head on his shoulder. In the living room, two of the observers stripped, their shirts and tops tossed aside before they disappeared, a motion that reminded Jason of swimmers diving into a pool.

Dan stuffed a twenty into the bartender's tip jar and handed out the same drinks they'd ordered in the bar on their first night together. A tall man saddled up to Arlene, a hug and then a hand extended to Dan. With him, a woman who rose onto tiptoes to muss Dan's hair. Jason guessed the streaks in her blond hair were blue, but the room's lights had him questioning his colors. Grunts and moans twisted into the stereo's wailing horn, the only living room bystanders now the naked ones who, exhausted and flushed, had pulled themselves from the maw. One, a tall woman with a faded C-section scar, walked unsteadily to the bar and ordered a shot of tequila.

Alice in her mask. The wetness in her eyes colored by the

room's blues and reds. Her gaze upon him. They could shiver in the cold until an Uber found its way into the sticks. He could insist Dan take them back, this fucked-up scene, the truth they'd failed to share. He tried to reach for her hand, but he was paralyzed, the momentum of their days, a weight he could trace back to the hotel bar, then back further still to the night Alice came to him with her secret about Roger. The world pressed upon him. The ocean's tides and the alignment of planets, and instead of reaching out, he donned his mask, the elastic's snap against the back of his head.

Arlene and the woman who may or may not have had blue hair laughed, their arms around each other. Another man joined them, and when Arlene introduced him to Alice, he kissed her hand. In the living room, a woman screamed, and they paused before rejoining their conversation. Dan at Jason's side. "This whole scene, it's not about sex. At least not all about it. It's about freedom, man. It's about celebrating a gift. This life, it's short, man. And this time, when our bodies aren't our enemies, is shorter still."

The woman from the living room screamed again: "Yes! Fucking yes!"

A man built like a linebacker took Arlene's hand. She set down her drink, a step from the bar before she reached back for Alice. The tall man and the woman with the blue hair followed. Halfway up the open stairwell, Alice glanced back, and Jason imagined how small he looked to her, another masked face amid the revelers.

A slender woman stepped to the bar. A short white dress, slits cut into its sides. Her hip pressed against Jason's. She smiled, asked if he'd order her a drink. Dan whispered in his ear, his breath warm with whiskey. "There's nowhere else a man can be so anonymous yet so completely present." The woman placed her hand on the small of Jason's back. Dan's voice so low it hissed: "Nowhere else a man can feel so completely fucking alive."

* * *

J ason caught his breath at the sidewalk's end. The snow a foot deep. Cars buried in white. The streets unpassable until the next plow. The storm had lasted through the night, and now, its last gasp, the plunk of sleet against his coat. A building breeze. Jason's snowblower gassed and ready to go, but he'd opted for his shovel. The physicality of the task. The chance to breathe unpoisoned air. To trade his house's silence for another kind of hush.

He came in for a drink, and in the vestibule, he stepped out of his boots, unzipped his coat. Alice on her laptop. Both of them logging in through the day. Zooms, conference calls. Emails. This modern life, and Jason thought of Fast Eddie and the turning wheel that took him nowhere.

Alice spoke, but not to him. Her earbuds in. The screen's anemic shine, and the colors took Jason back to last Sunday's comedown-morning light. The ride back to Baltimore. The windshield's grit and salt. Arlene slept. Twice Dan veered onto the shoulder before coming to with a shake of his head and a third-person admonishment to *keep it together, Dan.* In their hotel room, Jason and Alice showered then passed out in separate beds, sleeping until housekeeping woke them with the news that checkout was an hour ago.

In the four days since, they'd become sleepwalkers, passing each other in hallways, his nights on the couch, and if they hadn't argued, it was only because arguing would have required talking. That night in Jake's house, he'd filled his hands and senses—but here, on the other side of indulgence, he found a greater emptiness. An exile on his own island. The ocean that grew with each passing day.

He sidestepped her laptop's camera. A drink of water, and

112

he gazed out the window above the kitchen sink. In the yard, the neighbor's children. The drifts up to their thighs. Their bundled halos of hoods and caps. He thought of Sophie and a snow fort they'd built. Thick walls, a lawn tarp for the roof, filtered light beneath. Her christening—the blue palace, and they huddled inside. Jason's chattering teeth stilled until Sophie tired of speculating about the kingdom of the blue palace. All of it a fortune lost.

He stepped back into his boots. Outside, the deep white. His neighbor called her children. The wind kicked up, and from the roof, pinwheels of snow. He shoveled the walk's last stretch. The snow heavy, the strain in his back. He considered his house through exhaled breath. The blue palace had melted. Its princess had fallen beneath a tragic spell. In their grief, the king and queen were reduced to dust and tears. Having lost everything, all they had was each other. And once, where the king thought he might have found salvation, he understood there was only a mirror. His misdeeds and emptiness doubled. He and the queen outcasts from the world and from each other.

* * *

Jason in the front pew. This church of his youth, and the saints, serene and knowing and beautiful, looked upon him. These faces who knew the child praying beside his blind grandmother and later witnessed the prodigal's return, the murderer who'd almost confessed. At the altar's base, a coffin. He'd gone to her house after the blizzard. An afternoon of unreturned calls and texts. The door opened. His voice whittled in the still rooms. A child calling for his mother.

The organ played. *Help of the helpless, O abide with me.* Wind against the stained glass. The weatherman's warning of a polar vortex, frostbite, burst pipes. The hymn ended, *in life, in death, O Lord, abide with me.* The stained-glass light glistened on the coffin's wood, and in the silence, Jason thought of himself as a song's last note. His child gone. His mother. His father a mystery, a dark star, an orbit Jason had now inherited.

He bowed his head and closed his eyes. Alice beside him. Last week, he'd stood outside his snow-buried house, dwarfed by the wasteland behind his door and within his heart. They were done—he and Alice—although neither had said the words, and while they could put a thousand miles between themselves, they could never escape their past. He opened his eyes and stared into his clasped hands. The priest spoke. *Love. Eternity. Rest.*

And then, the day's sad irony—the small fortune he'd inherited. He'd handled his mother's finances for years, but she hadn't shared the totality of Bill's portfolio. The blue chips bought forty years ago. A sum five times Jason's debts. The money they'd squeezed from Roger made irrelevant. Enough to buy a dream house. Enough to buy a new life.

The priest called his name. Jason stood. His legs like water, and in the aisle, a sidestep of his aunt's wheelchair, her eyes upon him, understanding nothing. The altar steps, and above the candles and flowers, Christ on the cross, arms spread, a pose of flight, the anchoring of nails. Jason's shoes brushed over the red carpet, and he thought of the aquarium fish, rising, blind to the world above. The priest stepped aside, and at the rostrum, Jason unfolded the paper he'd pulled from his suitcoat pocket. A pause to collect himself. A look down upon the coffin, his aunt, Alice . . .

. . . and Sophie. Sophie in the seat he'd abandoned. Sophie in her Sunday dress, her eyes upon him. A heartbeat then another before he blinked and she was gone.

* * *

Jason stood by his office window. In the lot, Nathan's wheel-chirping Mustang led the charge to Friday's happy hour. An hour ago, Jason had received a call from his boss's secretary to schedule a meeting after work. He couldn't ask Madison what she knew, his life of burnt bridges. A trip to the vending machines near closing. Glances from the pit, the breakroom's hush, and Jason understood the blood in the water was his.

The pit quiet now. His boss's door open. Inside, his secretary gathered her coat and purse. An expression little different than the day the police came to question him. Little different than the parents of Sophie's old friends. The voyeurs. The crystal-ball gazers. The searchings of Jason's face for the fates they feared most. "He's waiting," she said, nodding to his door.

Jason stepped inside. Smith at his desk. Smith took off his glasses and invited Jason to sit. His office's glare replaced by winter's dusk. In the lot, the headlights of the straggling exodus, and Jason imagined how he looked to them. A still life behind glass. This lonely fish. His boss spoke, how this wasn't easy and he wished things were different. He shared some bullshit story of a man relegated to the pit who earned his way back into an office in less than two years. Nathan had earned his shot, and Smith was sorry but *business was business*.

Jason said little beyond *yes* and *I know* and *I understand*. He even shook Smith's hand because why not. Because the news meant little. Because they could have their hamster wheel. Because nothing touched him now—not sadness, not joy. Nothing.

He returned the next afternoon. His hands in his pockets, a shivering against the cold. The night's single digits and a sun

116

without warmth. He hadn't told Alice. He wanted to spare himself the pain of her indifference. Her shrug. The turn of her back. The two of them no longer lovers or husband and wife—they were simply sharers of space. Their house of echoes and memories. The cold that radiated from their snow-packed roof.

Jason shook the office key from his ring and deactivated the alarm. The place still, and he turned on the lights. The custodian had piled empty boxes outside his office door. Inside, Nathan's boxes. His framed college lacrosse jersey. A photograph of him shaking hands with Ben Roethlisberger. Jason took down his plaques and diploma. He saved his desk's framed photo, a clay penholder Sophie had made in third-grade art. What remained, he swept into a box, the same care taken when he upturned his drawers. A shower of pens and paper clips. His business cards. Aspirin for his knee. A faded purple scrap fluttered and settled between his shoes.

He sat, elbows on his knees, and unfolded the paper. Sophie's handwriting. A reminder to stop by the sporting goods store on his way home and pick up a new mouthguard. A joke about not ruining her teeth after three years of braces. A season she never got to finish.

He set his boxes on Nathan's cleared desk. This view he'd forgotten. The elevated walkway. The shut office doors. Silence, but beneath, he heard the pit's clucking stupidity. It's grind of money, money, money. On the computer monitor, a single Post-It. *No hard feelings*—Z. Jason slid his office keys off his ring and tossed them on the desk. His hands empty save the penholder, framed picture, and Sophie's note. He didn't intend to set off the alarm—but neither did he care. Fulbright and Smith just another wreck in his rearview, and he could no more return and make things right than he could spread his arms and fly into the clouds.

Jason rolled off Arlene, drained, his wild heart. The motel room eased back into focus. This world that had orphaned him, these days of lies and drift. The truth he kept from Alice. His aimless morning drives. Afternoon matinees. Extra cups of coffee at diner counters. Walks along the frozen river. A shadow in this life of useful men.

He'd called Arlene at work. She'd been hesitant at first; there were rules after all. Understandings. "You can't have openness without being *open*," she'd said, but he pressed, sensing some disconnect, some unspoken tension between her and Dan. Their reunion in the lobby of an anonymous beltway motel, a mingling with the continental breakfast crowd. He'd paid for two nights but would only stay for these stolen workday hours. The thick curtains drawn, and if he'd pulled them back, he'd have seen not the harbor view of their previous encounters but an industrial park's concrete and glass.

Arlene propped the pillows behind her and reached for her purse on the nightstand. She took a hit from her vape, shook it, and took another hit. She spoke, her voice pinched. "You're going to wear me out, lover boy."

"Thanks for meeting me."

She turned, looked down upon him. The unkind light. Above her, water stains on the ceiling. "Not a word to Alice."

"Not a word."

"How did you manage it?"

She took another hit, exhaled a faint cloud, and shook the pen again. "I just showed up here. You did all the planning and plotting and made the long drive. What will you say when you go home tonight?"

"I'll say I had a good day at the office."

She clicked the remote. A newscast, an update on the city's homeless, at least half a dozen dead in the cold snap. "And what will you say when you go back to work?"

He grabbed her wrist, the remote dropped, an arm around her waist. An old wrestling move, and in an instant, Arlene lay on her back, her black hair fanned over the pillow. She smiled at his roughness, and he said, "I'll tell them I'm feeling much, much better."

They kissed, slow and deep. He pulled back, and she ran a finger under his chin. "Alice told me about your Sophie." She rested her palm against his cheek. "I told her I'd pray for her. For all of you."

He should have been tired. The sex. The ride. He should have been hungry, but he wasn't. The dining room's quiet amplified by the scrape of her fork, the furnace's struggle to push back the cold. Seashell murmurings, close yet muffled. The temperature below zero, this the last and coldest night of the polar vortex. Alice considered him, her fork by her mouth. He watched her chew, and it pained him less to think of her fucking a stranger than to imagine her betrayal of their daughter.

Alice chewed, swallowed. "What's wrong?"

He couldn't tell her about Arlene or his job, but there was another truth he could share. He reached across the table and held her hand. His voice low, calm. "Remember the night we sat here and you told me about Roger and what he'd done?" He rubbed his thumb over the back of her hand. "Remember our worries about losing the house. The hospital. The fucking vampires from the insurance company. How unfair it all felt, how meaningless?"

She looked into his eyes.

"You know all about that night." He smiled. "You were here. It was your idea. You brought it into our lives, and I bought into it. But you don't know about that night in the garage. I never told you because I wanted to protect you. Because you couldn't tell the police about what you didn't know, but we're in the clear now, aren't we?"

"Jason." She tried to pull away. He squeezed harder.

"He came at me. He'd been drinking. He was angry. He didn't want to give us any more. He said if he got busted, he'd turn us in, too. He was back and forth, yelling, sobbing. All I wanted was to get out, to be done with him. He grabbed a wrench, and I stepped close, not wanting to give him room to swing, and when I did, I saw it in his face. He was sick. Paranoid. I just wanted to wrap him up and talk him down. But he swung."

Alice stood, and he did too. His grip secure. Her pulse against his fingers. His hip struck the table, and their water glasses toppled. She backed up, and he followed, the movement of dancers, back, back until she bumped into the kitchen counter. Water dripped from the table, a puddle on the floor. Outside, the wind's whistle. She tried to jerk free, and her futility pleased him.

"I went blank, just for a second. The way I'd done before when I got slammed to the mat. But I didn't let go, and when I came to, we were as close as we are now. Close enough to smell the gin on his breath. He was like a child. He was weak. And I told him I'd let him go if he dropped the wrench, but he wouldn't, and he kept trying to jerk free."

"Jason—"

She slumped, a slow melt, her back to the cabinets they'd once secured with plastic locks, Sophie so curious, always getting into things. He lowered himself with her, crouching, then kneeling. "It's OK, baby. It's OK because we don't have anything to fear anymore. That's what I was trying to tell Roger. Don't be afraid. Even though my head was throbbing. Even though I couldn't think through the static."

These past weeks, she'd made him invisible. Tonight, he was the center of her universe, brighter than the sun and all the stars. She began to tremble.

"And we moved like that. Him struggling. Me not letting go, trying to get him to calm down, to drop the wrench, and when we tripped, I wasn't sure if there was something on the floor or if our feet got tangled, but when we went down, we went down together. Me on top, and his head hit one of the stairs that led inside."

She looked away. "Please."

He cupped her chin, a squeeze, her pretty face contorted. "I felt the crack. Skull. Neck. I still feel it. I feel it now. And his mouth was next to my ear." He leaned in and pressed his cheek against hers. "Close enough to hear him gasp." He pulled back. "And when I pushed myself up, I watched the light fade from his eyes. Just the way we did with Sophie. Our beautiful Sophie."

He took her hand in his. Her face wet. Her words choked between sobs. "Why're you doing this? Why are you doing this to me?"

He brushed back her hair. "Because I love you, baby. Because we're in this, the two of us. All of it, now and forever."

* * *

The sky clear, moonless. The winter constellations Bill had taught him. The snow deep and blue. Ice on the sidewalk. The steam of his breath. Alice back home, their bedroom door locked. This life of frozen landscapes.

Nestled in his hand, a crowbar's curved head. The rest of the bar beneath his sleeve. He checked the street signs. This complex of townhouses upon townhouses. His steps quicker beneath the streetlamps. Then the street he was looking for. Most of the windows dark. These sensible people. The small hours after midnight, alarms set for dawn. He slowed as he approached the yellow Mustang.

He slid the crowbar from his sleeve. He'd come with one intention, but vandalism felt cheap on the heels of murder. He looked up and considered an unlit window, Nathan's bedroom perhaps. Jason remembered Sophie on the diving board, cannonballs into the deep end, and the moment turned inside-out—day for night, warm for cold, joy for emptiness—and here he was, a different man, yet the moment's physics remained the same. The waves that radiated from a sinking body. The ripples of memories and dreams.

And the moment turned inside-out again, and Jason saw himself from Nathan's window. A shadow against the snow. The realization that a locked door meant nothing to man who'd lost everything.

Jason woke in his daughter's bed. The room's heat off. The quilt Alice's mother had sewn clutched beneath his unshaven chin. The windows veined with frost. His cobwebbed thoughts. Cold dreams, labyrinths, rooms without escape. Alice gone for an overnight trip with her parents. An aunt in hospice. The turnpike's long hours and stretching forests. The midnight tunnels bored into the Alleghenies. There'd be no phone calls or texts from her. Jason alone in his abandoned orbit. The hollow ache that now accompanied the word *home*.

Downstairs, he checked the refrigerator, but there was little to eat. He made himself coffee and dressed. The car fob lifted from the vestibule's hooks, and on the last hook, Sophie's lanyard, a house key unused. The day's rhythms different after rush hour, retirees, housewives. The sun split the clouds, its sheen in the gutters' long icicles. He passed a church, a hearse parked in front, passed the snow-covered field where Sophie had played soccer. His phone buzzed, another call from Madison, her worry greater than her anger, but he didn't answer. He thought of a hotel in Baltimore and a hallway of locked doors. There was no turning back now.

The supermarket. The produce aisle's melons, and he remembered Alice, a joke, an invitation, his moans in the lot's shadowed rear. And he thought about movie gangsters in witness protection programs, and how their histories could be erased but not the prisons they carried in their hearts. Behind the deli counter, a man with a hairnet over his beard worked the slicer. The piling of cut meat, an act both mesmerizing and repulsive. A life snuffed. This thoughtless consumption.

He abandoned his cart. His appetite lost. An unhinging in

his knees. The fear he may collapse. The aisle's dreamy stretch, the assault of lights and cheery music and the shelves' bright boxes, and in his thoughts, the carp in his stepfather's boat. Their flailing. Their gaping mouths. His kind and kin.

He spotted her at the aisle's end. She held a bag of cookies, her mother—he recognized her as well, her tearful TV pleas—examining items on the opposite shelves. Jason slowed, and perhaps he really was dreaming, still asleep in Sophie's bed. The girl inched closer, her attention on Oreos, Chips Ahoy, one bag picked up and the other returned. This girl who'd been lost and prayed for. Who'd been returned from the dead. The purple and pink windbreaker he'd glimpsed beneath the game land's shifting leaves replaced by a bulky parka. But her hair the same, her eyes. He inched forward. Dreaming yet not, his lips parting. A desert in his throat.

"Honey," the mother said. She pushed her cart between Jason and her daughter. The girl's hand in hers. A glance as they hurried past.

* * *

Is return to Flannigan's unplanned. His drift. A roulette wheel's scuttling ivory ball. The street narrowed, the curb's hip-deep snow, but a space waited outside Flannigan's door. A welcoming. A homecoming. The inside's stink of smoke and spilled beer. The TV muted, a horse race no one bothered to watch. The bartender different, heavyset, a nod as Jason claimed a stool. The booths empty, the bar too save the old man who occupied the stool beneath the TV.

Jason ordered a shot and a beer. Another horse race started. Florida, perhaps California, towering palms and the kind of sunshine that seemed impossible on a winter's day. The old man rubbed his face. The TV's glow upon him. The horses turned the homestretch. The bartender coughed then spit into the backbar sink. Jason threw back his shot and signaled for another. He watched his glass fill. "One for the old man, too."

The old man looked up, and the bartender pointed to Jason. The old man lifted his glass, and Jason returned the gesture. The old man sipped, his lips smacking. The rest of the shot downed in a gulp. On the TV, handlers wrestled a skittish horse into its chute. The old man rose. A steadying hand on the bar. A shuffle toward Jason. "Thank you, son."

"My pleasure."

The old man cocked his head. A squint of bloodshot eyes. "I know you, don't I? I can't place it, but I know I do."

"Maybe. Maybe so."

The old man patted Jason's shoulder and shuffled toward the bathroom. "Then Godspeed, my boy. Godspeed."

* * *

Jason waited for Alice outside her office. The melting snowpack, puddles around his shoes. His breath steamed and faded into the mist. Others exited, men and women bundled in coats, and he wondered if any of them had thought about Roger today. Jason could have waited in the car, but he wanted Alice to see him. He had neither the words nor the right to ask for forgiveness, and if there was nothing left for him to say but goodbye, then at least he could do that with respect for what they'd once had. The effects of the drinks he'd had at Flannigan's had passed, and he was tired, heavy in his body but not in his thoughts. Not in the knowing of what he was doing was right. He straightened when he spotted her.

Alice held the door, and behind her, Arlene, and for Jason, a flashback. The supermarket aisle. The carp in his stepfather's boat. The inability to breathe. Alice clutched her collar, brushed the hair from her face. Arlene laughed, then Alice, but their smiles froze when they spotted him.

"Jason." She considered his jeans. "Did you leave work early?"

Arlene held her briefcase in front of her, a two-handed grip. "Hey there."

Alice gestured toward Arlene. "Arlene's up for some training today."

"Your wife has been very patient." Arlene smiled. "I'm not the best with new tech."

Jason smiled too. All of them acting. This mannered surface. Their ocean of secrets. He looked from Alice to Arlene and back to Alice, and his smile hardened because he sensed their unease. Their fear a coal, and its warmth filled him. A flush more intense than Flannigan's whiskey as he suggested the three of them grab dinner.

"It'll give you a chance to miss rush hour," he said. "There's construction on the interstate. It's a mess this time of night."

"That's true," Alice said.

The mall nearby, and in it, a Japanese steakhouse. Alice and Arlene each drove, Jason in the lead. The radio off. The carousel of his thoughts. In the lot, Arlene held up her palm. "Is that ice?" The mist heavier now, and woven into it, a thousand whispers. Halos beneath the lot's tall lights.

They shared a grill-side table with a young couple. The other tables empty, the early hour, the weather, and at the bar, one of the chefs drank with the hostess who'd seated them. The sake Jason ordered warm, clean, a bit sweet, and when they finished their first carafe, Jason ordered another. The grill's sizzle and heat, and their raised glasses saluted their chef. The flash of his knives. The egg cracked over a spatula. The onion volcano. The tossed shrimp and a round of applause when the young man caught it in his mouth, a kiss from his pretty girl-friend. Arlene's boisterous eruptions, and with them, the memory of their first night in Baltimore. Beside Jason, the beaming faces of his wife and the last woman he'd fucked, and when a flame jumped from the grill, their features blurred one into the other.

Jason picked up the tab, and buzzed with food and wine, they checked out the mall. The corridors' hush, the empty stores. The situation's awkwardness had faded, and when Arlene and Alice laughed over a pair of blond shag wigs, Jason bought one for each. Arlene found a mirror and put hers on, then Alice. "Twinsies," Arlene said. She puckered her lips, a kiss for their reflections then a peck for Alice's cheek.

Outside. The mist now a steady drizzle. The lot's cars

encased in dimpled cocoons. The walkway slick but salted. The macadam an ice rink, and they clung to each other, mincing steps, laughing then not. Alice slipped, Jason and Arlene on either side, holding her up, almost falling themselves. Decisions were made—Arlene would stay the night, their trip home in a single car, the others retrieved in the morning. The doors of Jason's car stubborn, and he tugged and cursed, his feet sliding beneath him, until he was able to open one. He let the engine run while he scraped. The ice chipped, a shower of flecks. First to come into view was Alice. Then the back window and a wave from Arlene in her wig.

The fifteen-minute ride took almost an hour. Their creep, hazards on. They skidded through stop signs. The numb glide as they spun, the windshield's unmoored panorama, the dreamy chaos. The mall's laughter gone, the silence punctuated by Alice's "Whoa" as she grabbed the dash. They passed a car halfway up a curb, another that had rear-ended a parked van. In the back, Arlene texted Dan. The ice, her plans to stay the night. She sighed, her thumbs tapping, an exchange that stretched longer than a sharing of information, and Jason thought about what she'd said the other day. Their troubles. The challenges of their kind of love.

Jason eased into their driveway. More slipping on the sidewalk. Alice and Arlene holding hands. The street's hush. Inside, relief and the shedding of coats. "Cozy," Arlene said when Alice started the fireplace. Arlene settled on the couch. "You have a beautiful place."

"Lines of sight," Jason said.

She looked over her shoulder then turned back. "Lines of sight indeed." She checked her phone then turned it off. "Looks like it's supposed to get above freezing in an hour or two. Either way, I don't think I'm driving tonight."

Alice rubbed her neck. "Could use a drink after that. Do we have anything?"

Jason kicked off his shoes. "Might be a couple beers in the back of the fridge."

"Think I need something stronger than beer." Alice put a CD into the player. "Wait, don't you have a bottle? The one you bought for that client in the nursing home?"

He thought of Mr. Keane, the old man fading, his worries about a lost son. "I'm not sure where it is."

"I think I know." Alice stood. "The study maybe."

She left. Arlene slid off her shoes. "That was some ride."

Jason sat, a chair close to Arlene's corner of the couch. It struck him as odd, this living, breathing space he occupied while the rest of the world lay captured in ice. "We're good, right? You and me?"

"Don't I seem good?"

"Yes. Yes you do. How about Dan?"

She shrugged. "Dan has his ways. I'm not always sure where his head is at."

Alice returned, a black box in hand. "Oh, that's the good stuff," Arlene said.

"Really?" Alice set the box on the coffee table.

"Top shelf." Arlene opened the box and held the bottle at arm's length as she read the label. "Your office knows how to gift, my boy."

Alice retrieved three glasses while Jason worked the stopper. The scent heavy. Thick. His father's smell, his breath, his sweat. Jason poured a few fingers for each of them, and they lifted their drinks, another toast, this one to the calm that follows fear. The burn in his throat. A wince for Alice. A shudder and a whoop from Arlene. Arlene and Alice on opposite ends of the couch. Arlene pulled up her feet and tucked them beneath her. Her skirt hiked above her knees. A peek of thigh. She made a joke about work tomorrow as she hit her vape. Jason next. His lungs filled, the women lost behind his exhale.

He sat on the floor and refilled their glasses. The fireplace warm on his back. The light on the women's faces. Alice shook the plastic bag, and the wigs flopped onto the coffee table. Arlene put one on and tossed the other to Jason. The elastic tight against Jason's brow, and he rubbed a hand through the hair. The cheap material. The light charge of static. He took it off, but when he tossed it back on the table, Alice snared it.

Arlene spoke over the rim of her drink. "You two are so fucking cute." Alice put on the wig. Once, Jason knew her thoughts, but he'd lost that vision. Alice took a hit off the pen then leaned over the coffee table, her face close to Jason's. Her nearness took him off guard, these weeks of distance. She exhaled into his mouth. The smoke wreathed their faces, a fog she punctuated with a kiss, and with the touch of her lips, her thoughts revealed themselves. She was punishing him, kissing him the way she kissed Dan. An emasculation. A show for Arlene. A territorial marking. Alice pulled back and stared into his eyes. A challenge, a dare. Arlene's voice from behind. "Don't let me stop you two."

Alice pushed aside the coffee table and joined him on the floor. They knelt, undressed each other, both of them—he was certain—self-conscious yet assured, actors who knew their roles better than their hearts. The heat in her kisses rooted not in his touch but in this new set of eyes, this audience and its history. He allowed her to dictate, and she guided his hands, his hips, losing herself in the charade. She wasn't his wife but another woman, anonymous in her wig—anyone, no one. She pushed him to the floor and straddled him. Her climax shuddering and profane. Her fingernails digging into his sides and the firelight upon her.

She climbed off, but before she could get far, he latched onto her arm and brought her to her hands and knees. Her head down, the arrow of her spine lined toward Arlene. His turn now, and his body worked with a slow, ramping violence. Arlene bit her lip. When Alice's wig fell off, Jason snatched her hair, a yelp he ignored, her head lifted, a presenting of her pained face to Arlene as he came deep inside her.

He slumped back and sat on his haunches. Alice rose on shaking legs. She picked up her wig and let it drop on the coffee table. Arlene sipped her drink. "Well, that was more entertaining than anything I could have found on TV." Jason thought of his stepfather's cabin, the summers he could swim across the lake, and how he'd rest, sitting like this on the opposite shore. Alice slid into her blouse but didn't button it. Her knees red. Her eyes empty. She finished her drink and went upstairs to get Arlene some pillows and blankets.

Jason stood. He used his undershirt to wipe his thighs and balls. Arlene offered the vape, but he waved her off. "You were on fire there, lover."

"It hasn't been like that. Or it was, then it wasn't."

"But it was tonight?"

He gathered his clothes. "It was."

Arlene smiled. "Wonder why."

Alice returned. Blanket and sheets, a pillow, a T-shirt and flannel pants. The firelight in the glasses' wet bottoms until Jason shut the valve and snuffed the flames. Alice and Arlene tucked in the sheet while Jason cleared the glasses. The women discussed the alarms they'd set, the downstairs shower Arlene could use, and when Alice went upstairs, Jason followed. Arlene fluffed her pillow. "Night, you two."

Alice used the bathroom then Jason. He cupped his hands beneath the spigot, drinking, splashing his face. The toilet's gurgle as he took a long piss. Alice in bed, her back to him, the blankets pulled tight. He settled in, touched her shoulder. "Please, don't," she whispered. He lay on his back, his eyes opened, the ceiling lost in the dark, and he imagined the roof, the burial of snow, then the deeper burial beneath the winter night. He wondered what would happen to their secrets when he left. Wondered if, unburdened from each other, they'd be free to lock their sorrows into another sealed room, the dust stirred only when they stepped inside. Or had the weight they'd carried actually been halved all along, and without Alice, might he crumble beneath the load.

He drifted. The ashy reach that comes before dreams. A moment's peace but then his daughter's voice, and he resurfaced into his bed. Alice asleep, or pretending to be. He was thirsty, the alcohol and the weed the house's dry heat. He pulled on his sweats and crept downstairs.

Arlene dozed on the sofa. The wigs tangled on the coffee table, and Jason thought of the drawer of Sophie's headscarves, the colors to match any outfit. He filled a glass at the sink and drank. One glass, then another, and he couldn't remember the last time water tasted so good. This humble act, a cleansing, and might it be this simple? This asking and receiving. The salvation waiting on the other side of surrender, so close and at hand, and perhaps all he had to do was give over. To God. To man. To a force beyond logic and language—but so much was a blur, and he couldn't think beyond the moment let alone to the other side of dawn. He filled the glass again, and Arlene entered the kitchen, barefoot, a hand mussing her hair. "You're reading my mind."

She wore one of Alice's college T-shirts, and beneath, the push of her breasts. He handed her his glass. The room dim, the green hue of the stove and microwave clocks. Their hands touched as he took back the glass. She wiped water from her chin, and he leaned forward and kissed her. Soft at first, tender, and how different her kiss was from Alice's. The wetness of her mouth, her tongue's curl. Here, in this touch, he understood why Alice had accepted their offer that first night. This chance to hold yourself close to someone who didn't know you. The chance to be someone different. Someone new. Someone you didn't hate when you looked in the mirror.

She rubbed his cock until he was hard. "Hold on a second, darling." She left then returned, naked outside her T-shirt and the wig atop her head.

He lifted her onto the kitchen counter. She laughed, the counter's chill, and with a bit of maneuvering, he entered her. "That's my boy," she cooed. From the cabinets, the soft clatter of plates. But the position proved awkward, its tip-toed angle, his fumbling aggravated by his desperation.

"Let's try something different here, love." Arlene slid off the counter, but before she could return to the living room, he grabbed her waist. He needed her. He was drowning. Drowning in lies. Drowning in death. He bent her over the breakfast table, his hands on her hips, the shirt bunched up her back. A tuft of black hair escaped the wig. The tile cold on his feet. In the patio doors, their faint reflection. The crouching night and the yard's snow. The two of them etched in black and white. The table shook.

He left his body. A vision-movie, a story that belonged to his eyes but not his mind, not his heart or gut. The doors' muted reflection, two grunting animals. He began to go soft. He closed his eyes, the movie projector sputtering, but as hard as he thrust, he couldn't claw his way back into the moment. He staggered back, and Arlene stood. "You OK?" she whispered.

"Just got a flash. A little dizzy." He gripped the counter, his watery knees. "I'm not used to drinking so much."

She filled the glass at the sink and handed it to him. She

pulled a chair from the table. "Why don't you catch your breath?"

He laid a steadying hand upon the table and sat. Sparks across his eyes. The hum of electricity, the wires buried behind walls and beneath his feet.

Arlene laid a hand against his cheek. "You OK, baby?"

She left then returned. The flannels back on, vape in hand. She paused at the picture Sophie had drawn. A house with three windows, a face in each. She lifted the frame from the wall, and her exhale broke over the glass. "She must have been a precious thing."

He leapt to his feet. A momentum as sure as falling, only there was no bottom, no earth, and just as he had at Sophie's graveside, he fell and fell, and only his hands upon Arlene's throat saved him from the yawning pit. Shaking. Squeezing. Arlene's mouth open yet silent. The wig slid over her eyes. Her free hand clutched his wrist, her fake nails, his real blood, and he couldn't let go any more than he could stop falling, and perhaps this was hell, a forever plummet, his heart on fire and the blackness all around—

She dropped the picture, and the glass shattered at their feet. He let go, the spell broken, and she staggered back. Her hip struck the refrigerator, her body bent, one hand on the countertop, the other on her throat. "Fucker," she said, a voice like sand.

He stepped back, and then a wince. He lifted his foot and pulled out a glass shard. Blood on his fingers, sticky, warm. In the living room, he fumbled into his clothes. He had no thoughts beyond escape—this house, this night, his shadow. He grabbed his coat and keys, his shoes untied. A vase flew past his head and shattered on the fireplace's stone.

"Fucker!" Arlene gasped. Her hand on her throat. The

words strained. The wig in a crazy angle atop her head. "I'm calling the cops, you motherfucker!"

Alice's sleepy voice: "Jason?" Then frightened: "Jason?"

He started the car. The ice now rain, yet the macadam remained slick. A fishtail out of the driveway. A slam into a neighbor's car. An alarm's wail as he sped away.

* * *

His wipers slapped. Ice clung to the cars and trees, a sheen beneath the streetlights. The dash's temperature display above freezing and inching higher. Here and there, a slick spot, the connection of road and rubber lost. He passed a familiar billboard. A little girl's face, and beneath, a pasted addition: *Welcome home!* Backroads, the sprawl abandoned. Pastures and fields, the bone-white snowpack. Twice he lost control, but he didn't question himself, his only map the places he couldn't return to. His soul's broken compass. He thought of his mother, a morgue's slab, the grave that would be dug with the thaw. He thought of Sophie waiting for her beneath the snow. His foot pressed heavier on the gas.

He should have grabbed the money, the gun, but how does one flee a house on fire? He was dead. Dead in hope. Dead in spirit. Dead in all but his body's mundane flicker of pumps and bellows. All those who'd held him in their hearts were gone, and in the hearts that remained, the poison of his words and deeds.

An hour passed, then another. This world of dreamers. The narratives which, upon waking, slipped like water through his fingers. Every dawn an exile and a reunion. He understood where he was going now. The pull of years. The fate to which he'd been blind. But now he saw the light, halleluiah and amen. The tears he wiped away ones of relief. Of deliverance.

He slowed, not wanting to miss the turnoff. The snow deep on the spur, and he could only plow through a few yards before getting stuck. He killed the engine. A breeze, and from the woods, the chime of shed ice. The chain that blocked the spur lost in the snow. He trudged down the spur, his feet lifted high, the crunch of the pack's iced crust. The wetness in his shoes. The numbness creeping through him.

To his left, a snap and a splintering crash, a branch unable to bear its weight. His trudging turned difficult, and he stopped to catch his breath, and he was wrong about being alive in only the working of heart and lungs. He was alive in pain and the hatred of the man he'd become. Alive in his relief that he was done lying to the world. Done with the creak of his nowhere-wheel. He stumbled. The drifts. The pack's crust. His jacket open and the flaps lifted on the breeze. He reeled back to a lost summer. This stretch, shaded and warm. The car windows opened and Alice by his side. A weekend getaway. The days of health and love he was too ignorant to cherish. The belief the world was waiting to hear their voices. Then their visits with Sophie. This new set of eyes. A reminding of wonder.

He entered the clearing. The trees pulled back. Above, masked by the dark, the scuttle of clouds, a river of wind. The cabin a shadow, and he could go inside. He could warm himself by the fire. He could sleep. Instead, he stumbled on until he stood at the lake's edge.

He was tired—he hadn't realized how tired. In the east, dawn's gray sliver. A sunrise he couldn't outrun. Along the lake, sculpted drifts. He was cold, and beneath his jacket, the chill of sweat. Tired and cold. Cold and tired. The world presented itself in great dueling swaths—light and dark, yes and no, up and down, alive and dead—and he was thankful for the clarity, and here, finally, was his religion. A belief truer than his meager understandings. He stepped from the shore. The snow not as deep on the ice. The unblocked wind, dunes that curled and rose and dropped, a maze both thoughtless and beautiful. The shoreline trees swayed, and their bony echoes carried across the ice, and from their skeletons, a flight of birds, so many the sky rippled then tore in two. He staggered but didn't fall. Beneath him, the water's buried pulse. A thousand sleeping fish.

The ice groaned as he neared the lake's center. This was the stretch he swam as a teen. Then again, not so long ago. Their last trip here as a family. His pace slow, and not far off, Alice and Sophie in the rowboat. Sophie's headscarf as blue as the sky. He swam to distract them from their worries. Swam to show her he'd be strong for her. He wasn't the young man who first conquered this stretch, and there were moments of exhaustion and doubt. Moments when he heard his father's voice. *Shitbird. Hey, Shitbird.* He pushed on, the oars' pulse in the water. The voices of Alice and Sophie when he lifted his face to breathe. Finally, the shore, its salvation and exhaustion. Smiles. The three of them lingering in the sun's warmth. He was a good man once. He was. He was.

A crack. Then another. The fissures in the ice yet also within him. The song in his bones, his teeth. On and off. Black and white. Day and night. Alive and dead. Another step and another crack. This thin margin, and he was a good man once, and he was sorry, so sorry. He approached the shore, and the trees rose, taller and taller, and in their branches, curious birds. Their songs greeting the sun and this strange creature upon the ice.

He stopped. God, the elements—whatever force painted the moment, he wanted to give it time to claim him, but even the birds fell silent, and he stood alone beneath this deaf heaven. He breathed into the stillness. Waiting. Inviting. Begging.

III

* * *

The cape's southernmost lifeguard, the one nearest the Point and the lighthouse, is the first to blow his whistle. One by one, the other guards rise from their whitewashed perches and join the chorus, the shrill cry carried on the breeze. At the surf's edge, mothers and fathers gather the children who've spent the afternoon collecting shells and pebbles as smooth as glass. Another day is done.

Jason wipes down the returned umbrellas and chairs, empties the water cooler, the ice he bought this morning reduced to melt and slivers. He takes down the flags and pennants that have serenaded him all day with their rippling *tsk-tsk-tsk*. The crowd thins, a ragtag exodus, refugees, some pulling wagons with oversized wheels, others laden with blankets and coolers, chairs and boogie boards. Barefoot children hurry-step over the hot sand, the adults lagging behind, their expressions dulled by heat and exhaustion. Jason offers a good evening to the lifeguards, boys half his age, then sets off to collect the unreturned umbrellas that bear the yellow-and-blue logo of Dom's Rentals.

When he's done, Jason secures the shed and sets out on his evening walk. The shoreline's sand the color of concrete, and the lapping waves erase his footprints. Months ago, on the shore of his stepfather's lake, he kicked aside the snow and curled into himself, waking into a gloom he believed to be evening, but, with the building light that greeted his trek around the lake's circling road, he soon realized was another dawn. Hungry, half frozen, he set out, driving until he ran out of road in this little shore town.

The sun inches toward the bay. Seagulls hover and land then take flight as he nears. He passes dog walkers. A father who snaps a picture of his identically dressed children upon a lifeguard's tower. The day's white clouds shade pink in the waning light, the sky's calm unmirrored in a surf that's rumbled all day, the lifeguards busy with their whistles and warnings, and Jason pictures the stirrings beyond the horizon. The storms and currents. The push of deep water. In the distance, a long cargo ship, and for Jason, the shifting perspectives of near and far. His old life a dream. Arlene and Dan. The divorce in which he'd granted Alice everything she'd wanted. The cold he woke to on the lake's snowy shore. The groan of ice waiting beneath every sandy step.

In town, the restaurants are filling. The day's second act, the waitresses and cooks, the tourists' sunburns and the cool touch of white sheets. Jason walks on. Far ahead, the light-house. Sometimes he swims after work, a glide through the calm beyond the breakers, but this evening, the surf is too rough. Anyway, he enjoys walking, these miles at the edge of the world. The dwarfing of sky and sea. The unblocked wind and pounding waves. The feeling of being both singular and consumed. He thinks, as he often does, about Roger and these days he's missed. He thinks about Arlene and the rage that blinded him. He thinks about Alice and hopes she's well. He passes the last lifeguard tower. The lighthouse a cylinder of white against the blue. Here, in this openness, in this great cathedral, his heart fills with forgiveness for everyone but himself.

Two boys sprint by. He's seen them before, locals, their lack of tags and proper beachwear. He figures the boys to be ten or so, and they engage in a running duel, each with a stick, their bare feet kicking up sand, their screams and the clack of wood overtaken by the surf as they hurry past. Jason stops to consider the waves. He and Alice and Sophie used to come here every July—perhaps this was the gravity that called him as he drove that frigid day. During the afternoon lull when business is slow, he sits outside the rental shack and listens, the breeze that weaves the beach's voices into a tapestry, the threads lifting, a word or two before returning to the hum, and in these moments, he feels Sophie near. This place she loved. The all and everything of sky and sea a more fitting frame than a cemetery's cold stone.

One of the boys who ran past charges into the surf but is knocked back. His stick swept away. He rights himself and yells into the waves: "Stevie! Stevie!"

The boy fifteen yards down shore. His friend gone, an erasure so complete Jason questions whether he saw him at all. Beyond the breakers, a face, a moment's glimpse. There's no flailing, no cry, just a shared heartbeat before the boy sinks beneath the surface.

Jason races into the water. A surge knocks him back, and he gathers himself then dives headfirst into a wave's curl. The roar in his ears. The darkness. The push so strong it steals his breath, and he emerges, gasping, beyond the breakers. On the shore, the other boy gestures, pointing, saying something Jason can't hear. Two women with their dogs run to the boy. Jason turns, fighting the current. Nothing. Just the surface's gray and the weight beneath. Just the lowering sun and the water he blinks from his eyes. Nothing, and panicked, he waves and kicks, a blind man's prayers, and when his foot meets something solid, he sucks a deep breath and goes under.

He opens his eyes, a reflex, a fool's belief in vision, the reality of darkness. His arms flail. The pressure ratchets in his chest until he's forced to surface. He goes down again, and he can feel the current's split, the pulse that carries him to shore and, beneath, the undertow, and in the dark flicker between them, he brushes the boy's face, his hair rising into Jason's fingers, and he grabs, first the hair, then an arm. He lifts, this underwater dance. The boy slips, and Jason gasps, the water rushing into his throat, his nose, before he breaks the surface.

Swells slap his face. Sand in his eyes, between his teeth. The boy held tight, the struggle to keep his face above water, the struggle to save the two of them from going down together. They near the shore, and when his feet rejoin the land, he's knocked to his knees. The world lost. The backwash's dizzying rush and the sting of pebbles and shells. The two women run to him, one lifting the boy, the other with an arm around Jason, who collapses, coughing and retching, onto the sand. One woman holds the boy around the waist and the other slaps his back. The boy blue-skinned, his body limp until he spits up and opens his eyes with a shudder.

Jason stands, his legs heavy and distant. Blood on his shins. The boy sitting now, his arms folded atop his raised knees, his head resting in his elbow's nook.

"He OK?" Jason asks.

The women sit on either side of the boy, each rubbing his back. The boy crying, his friend, too. The woman nearest Jason looks up. "I think, yes. Thank you."

Jason pictures what might follow. An ambulance. The police. A reporter. "Can you take it from here?"

"I think so," the woman says.

The boy looks up, blinking, and Jason smiles. "Glad you're OK, buddy."

He walks off. The waves roll over his feet, a gentle washing, yet in the touch, the memory of how lost and afraid he'd been in the dark just off shore.

* * *

He sets out on his bike, passing in and out of the morning's mist. The bike a yard-sale find. Its frame corroded, a sagging chain. The pace of decay here catches Jason by surprise. Metal rusts and paint peels and drains clog—and if he listens closely, he can hear the creak of a thousand hamster wheels beneath the surf.

He passes St. Brendan's. St. Brendan, the patron of mariners and all souls at sea. The church half the size of St. Mark's. A stained-glass window of an open boat, a man extending a hand to another swept into the waves. The priest, broom in hand, shoos sand from the vestibule steps. They've seen each other a few times like this. The street's morning hush, the syncing of routines and habits. The men nod their hellos, and Jason pedals on.

Later, he sits inside the rental shack. The doors opened wide. The sky mirrors the ocean's gray, and from time to time, the drizzle whispers upon the tin roof. The beach quiet but not empty. In his lap, the sketchbook he keeps in his backpack, and his pencil scratches as he draws the four boys who've spent the past week playing paddleball on a claimed spot near the shack. Their hours-long *plunk-plunk-plunk*, a rhythm that will disappear at week's end when they pack their things and go home. The boys quiet, focused, athletic. The game not serious so much as respected, and as he draws, Jason counts their volleys —ten, twenty, more. He possesses little artistic talent, yet each day, he draws, sometimes labeling his work with a line or two of narrative, snapshots, frames for moments otherwise lost. Sometimes he draws a single person, sometimes a vista of umbrellas. Sometimes he draws the ocean, which he's learned changes from day to day. He thinks of the children who dip strainers in

147

the surf, the filtering of sand, the treasures beneath, and he pictures a day in the future when he'll return to these pages, and he wonders what he'll remember and what he'll discover anew.

He gets the feeling he's being watched. The observer observed. He hears whispers before two boys and a woman step into view. One is the boy who shouted his friend's name from the shore. The other, the one clutching the woman's hand, is the boy Jason assumes is Steven, although he can't be sure. The boy he pulled from the water pale. Seaweed in his hair. His eyes crusted with sand.

"Told you." The boy who's not Steven points to Jason. "You're him, aren't you, mister?"

The woman, dressed in the orange and white of the shore's largest pizza chain, nudges the boy forward. The boy extends a hand. He's burly, wide in the chest, yet his voice is small. "Thanks, mister."

Jason shakes his hand. "Glad I was there."

The boy smiles. "Me, too."

"He ran right in." The other boy looks to the woman. "And for a while, they were both gone. I was yelling like crazy, then those two ladies with the dogs came running."

The woman offers her hand. She's younger than Jason, black hair, brown eyes. A butterfly tattooed on her wrist. "Both of us wanted to thank you. I don't know what—"

Steven, no longer bashful, steps in front of the woman. "Were you scared? I was scared. Really scared."

"Some, sure." He assumes the boy and the woman are mother and son. The eyes they share, their mouths. "Maybe more scared afterward."

Steven nods. "That makes sense." He fiddles with the lock on the shed door until his mother lays a hand on his shoulder.

"Arthur here is my friend." The other boy waves. "He said he recognized you. That's how come we found you."

"You ride that red and white bike," Arthur says.

"That's true."

Steven says, "And when he said that, I knew who he meant because I've seen you too. And I've seen that bike locked up behind the ice cream shop."

"We call it the candy-cane bike," Arthur says.

"That's a good name for it," Jason says.

"We live around the corner from the ice cream shop," Steven says. "Above the drug store."

"Then we're neighbors, aren't we?"

"Yeah," the boy says. "I guess we are."

"Let's let the man get back to work." The woman's hand on the boy's shoulder again, and Jason infers her history of gentle corralling, the boy's darting eyes and busy hands. "Thank you again. I don't know what I would have done." She trails off. Her expression frozen for a moment. "My name's Dee. Denise, really, but everyone calls me Dee."

They shake again. "Jason."

"I'll keep an eye out for the candy-cane bike," she says.

Later, the rain picks up. Jason brings in the shack's flags and pennants. The beachgoers gather their things, their urgency escalating as the rain grows heavier. Jason helps an old woman, chasing down an open umbrella that tumbles on the breeze. He returns to the shack. He's drenched, and around him, the mildewed scent of wet canvas. The rain falls in sheets, the shack's echoes. He keeps the doors open. His sketchbook on his lap. His pencil scratching. This empty beach and a horizon of a thousand grays.

* * *

Three days pass before Steven returns. A beautiful Saturday. A heatwave inland, but along this narrow strip, a breeze. All day, the snap and flutter of the shack's flags. The beach crowded. Jason's busy as the lifeguards blow their end-of-the-day whistles, and he turns from cleaning and stacking and bumps into Steven. The boy beams. A stained T-shirt. The cut-off shorts he wore the day Jason pulled him from the ocean. "Hey there, Mr. Jason."

"Hey, buddy."

Jason lifts a returned umbrella over the boy's head. More returns follow, and in the shack's cramped interior, he sidesteps the boy. Gone is the other day's shyness, and in its place, a barrage of questions and observations. How hot it is in town and did he see the sharks that closed the beach yesterday and how could the moon affect the tide during the day?

Jason sets out to collect the unreturned umbrellas and chairs. The boy at his side. His dollar-store flip-flops. His laughter as he chases scavenging gulls and his cowering dance as they caw above this head. Jason twists an umbrella from the sand. "People are supposed to bring them back on their own, aren't they?" the boy asks.

"Supposed to."

"That doesn't seem right."

"Guess it's a minor crime, as far as crimes go." Jason closes the umbrella. The boy looks at him, and in his gaze, a need, not for money or things, but to be seen. "You feel like helping out?"

"Sure."

He hands the boy the umbrella. "Take this back and lean it against the shed with the others."

The boy's chest swells. "OK." He snatches the umbrella

and takes two running steps before Jason calls, "No running while you're carrying that, chief. Got to be careful."

"I will." Steven's steps turn clipped and quick, and after he stands the umbrella beside the shack, he runs back but stops halfway. "Is it OK if I run without an umbrella?"

"That's fine."

"Cause that's what I did."

Jason hands him another umbrella, and they work this way until Jason hauls the last four himself, the boy by his side, his repeated askings if Jason needs help. As they near the shack, Jason spots Betty. Her straw hat and oversized sunglasses. A blue scarf that lifts on the breeze. Betty's husband Dom passed seven years before, but his name lives on in the rental shacks he'd established from the Point to Seaside Heights. Another of his holdings: the apartments above the ice cream shop, Jason a tenant before he was an employee, and since his arrival, he's come to know Betty a conversation at a time. Her Philadelphia roots and her family's summers at the shore. Then the Fourth of July she fell in love with an ambitious local boy, a hustler and a dreamer and a hopeless romantic. Their forty-three-year marriage, and her inheritance of his business after the stroke that felled him mid-sentence. The hints she's shared—the desire to be free of the shacks' hassles, the nickel-and-dime margins, the frustrations of dealing with teens who care more about evenings' parties than opening on time.

"Didn't know you hired a coworker," she says.

"I'm not a coworker, really," Steven says. "I'm just helping out."

"It's a long story." Jason sets down his umbrellas and turns to Steven. "Thanks, buddy. I'll see you around, OK?"

"I'll look for the candy-cane bike," the boy says. He runs off, turning once to wave from atop the dune.

"A long story?" Betty asks.

"A long story. I get the impression he's a little lonely." He wipes down a chair and returns it to the shed. "How're you doing?"

She sighs. In her dark lenses, the shoreline's crumbling waves. "I'm hoping you can help with a situation. The kid at 14th Street is out for the week. Maybe more. Left a message how his head wasn't in a good place. Like anyone's is these days." Fourteenth Street the next shack north, less than half a mile. "Do you think you could bike back and forth and juggle here and there until I find someone or he comes back?"

"Sure."

"Thanks." Her finger bothers an umbrella's tasseled fringe. "These kids and their dramas. I'm not cut out to be a fucking den mother."

* * *

He prepares dinner. This small apartment above the ice cream shop, a kitchen where he can't open the stove and the refrigerator at the same time. A simple meal—pasta, a few fresh scallops, salad. He's trimmer, the gym abandoned for nightly push-ups and sit-ups, for his post-work walks and swims, the miles he logs on his bike. He owns a radio but not a TV, and he feels better for it. He brings his plate to the couch. A library book on the coffee table, his quest to read the novels he faked his way through in college. The stray cat he found by the alley dumpster leaps up and settles beside him.

He's showered, but he still smells of sunscreen. He can't say he's happy, but his days' simplicity makes his shadow feel less deep. No one here knows the truths buried in his heart—the people he's hurt, the ones he misses. Alone in this cramped apartment, he speaks to them all. Apologies. Longings. Sometimes he feels not so much that he's run away but simply cleared out his life in order to stand naked before these ghosts.

He cleans up. His window open, and from the street, the evening's chorus. Cars and horns. The ice cream shop's traffic, the bell that rings each time the door opens, the sugary scent of homemade cones. Later, the avenue's closing-time crowds, drunks, college kids, most of their fun good-natured, but every so often, the nights he wakes to a broken window or a fist-fight's screams, the scatter of running feet as the sirens close in. Jason stretches out, his skin warm against the sheets. He cries, but not as much as he does some evenings. Long after the bars have closed, he wakes into silence. The streetlights angle toward his ceiling, the feeling of being submerged. The street hushed. The surf's crumble as steady as his breath.

153

* * *

Jason opens the 14th Street shack and takes care of the day's first customers. The smells and layout identical to his, the upkeep sloppier. The floor's empty water bottles. A phone number scribbled inside a match pack and a shell necklace, its latch broken, in the cashbox. Jason finds the sun-faded plastic tag Dom must have purchased years ago, a clock with poseable hands. *We'll be back at—*. Jason sets the hands to 11:00, but they sag to six-thirty.

He bikes to his shack. Haze over the water, a pale sky, a day destined to be hot. A land breeze, and on it, the bay's fishy scent. The flies and gnats thick. These past two days of washed-up jellyfish. His first hour busy. He accompanies his customers to their chosen spots, a weaving between blankets and tents, then jabs and twists the poles into the sand. He accepts the vacationers' tips and wishes them a good day. He's comfortable with the solitude he's found amid the crowd. A parade of strangers. The families he sees for a few days before they disappear. The ones who'll return next year, their children older, this place unchanged, everything predictable save Jason's place in the equation.

He pedals back to 14th Street, stopping along the way for a bag of ice, which he places in the bike's wire basket, and the case of water he balances atop that. He opens the shack, apologizing to the handful of waiting customers. The heat builds. Back and forth he goes, doing his best to adjust the time on the signs' clocks with the band-aids he discovered in the shack's first-aid kit, blinking away the gnats that grow thicker as the hours pass. Early afternoon, the usual lull busier after the jellyfish return and the lifeguards blow their whistles. Upon his arrival at his regular shack, Jason finds Steven sitting in the

154

structure's slim shade. The boy stands, wiping sand from his cutoffs.

"I was worried about you."

Jason opens the lock and swings back the doors. "I'm taking care of another stand too."

The boy walks into the shack. His fingers trace the umbrellas and chairs. A respectful inventory. "This is cool, huh?" The waves and wind echo, the shack's tin-can acoustics. "Should I stay and help again? Because I was helping while you were out."

"Helping how?"

"A couple folks returned things. I'll show you." He leads Jason to the shack's other side where he's propped a few umbrellas and chairs. "They said they were leaving early because of the jellyfish. And the smell." He pauses, sniffs, shrugs. "Anyway, I took off my shirt and wiped their stuff down. The way you do. Not with your shirt, but you know what I mean."

Jason extends his fist, and the boy gives it a bump. "Thanks."

The boy beams. "You're welcome."

Jason sets up two chairs in the doorway's shade. The boy talks, then he doesn't. Jason takes out his sketchbook, he and the boy side by side, taking in the sights and sounds. Partners on this imperfect day.

* * *

S ome evenings, when the sun angles low, Jason leaves out a single umbrella and follows his shadow into the surf. Beneath the umbrella, his shirt and sandals and towel. The water laps his shins, and in the tide, the scratch of sand and shells, his feet buried. These eons of churn and erosion.

He wades deeper. He turns, allows a wave to break over his back, and in its backwash, he dives in and emerges beyond the breakers. The world falls away, and he bobs for a moment before setting off. He swims parallel to the shore. A slow crawl. He lifts his face, making sure he's not drifting out to sea or about to tangle with a fisherman's line. He pictures his heart, this hidden pump, the rhythm beneath every song he knows, and in the ocean, he understands his heart's billion beats are just a single drop. A grain of sand. He thinks of the ocean, the sky, and wonders if, within him, he carries some flicker of the infinite.

When he nears the jetty's black rocks, he allows the tide to carry him to shore. The water pulls away, his feet on the slope's wet sand. He sits, tired in the best possible way, the ocean's rhythms in his meat, and catches his breath. He feels clean, new, and for a moment, he stands outside his sins. But then the moment fades, and he returns to the knowing of what he's done and who he is. Before he begins the walk back, he turns. The lighthouse's white shaded yellow. The day's light its most beautiful before the dark.

* * *

Another hot morning, his bike tires in need of air. Sand and broken glass on the road's shoulder. He walks the bike over the dune but drops it when he sees the shed's opened doors and a man walking away with an umbrella. He runs, half-stumbling across the sand, only to find Betty counting out change for the next customer.

"Hey," he says.

Betty in her sunglasses and straw hat. "Kid's not coming back, I guess. I'll put up some help-wanted signs. It's late in the season, though." She takes a water from the cooler and twists the cap. "It's changed, how kids look at work."

Jason nods. "I guess."

"I don't understand it." She sips. "But I don't begrudge them either. This is one messed up world we've left them."

She proposes an arrangement—she'll work the stand its first and last hour. In between, Jason can shuttle back and forth, and this evening, she'll buy them new signs to post in their absence, ones where the clocks' hands stay in place.

"This business. I hate it sometimes." She pauses then extends her hand, a showgirl's sweeping flourish. "But like Dom always said, 'Can't beat the view.'"

The breeze ruffles beneath the umbrellas. The hazy melt of sea and sky. "It is nice," Jason says.

"This was our first shack. Not this actual shack—that got washed away in '92—but this spot. Dom built it from the scraps they left behind when they tore down the old convention center." She takes off her hat, wipes her brow. "He was an insurance salesman with a surfer's soul. To be honest, he wasn't good at either. Never got as rich as he'd dreamed, but he spent his days out here. That was all he wanted. I should have told

157

him more how much I admired that." She takes another sip. "What's your story, Jason? Big picture. Men your age who just show up here are either lost or in trouble. Or both."

His reflection in her sunglasses, and he thinks of Alice, their bedroom, a frigid night. *I'm lost. So lost.* From the beach, the lifeguard's whistle, a wandering swimmer waved in. "I lived a regular life," Jason says. "Had a good job, a house."

"What kind of work did you do?"

"I was in finance."

She twists her mouth. "The police aren't looking for you, are they?"

"No. No one's looking for me."

The lifeguard blows his whistle again. He stands, his arms waving. Betty says, "I'm glad you're not in trouble. The being lost part—who isn't, at least a little." Another sip. "At least you picked a pretty place to do it."

* * *

L abor Day comes and goes, and with its passing, new rhythms. The shacks' slow days. The voices of children thinned from the breeze. The mornings cooler and the sunsets earlier, but the water still warm. A change in town as well. School busses. The diners' empty booths. His apartment windows open, but gone are the midnight revelers and the honking traffic, the nights peeled back to the pulse of traffic and crashing waves.

Betty arrives as he's about to gather the day's unreturned umbrellas. She tells him next weekend will be their last for the season. She shares her plans for her annual fall trip with a group she calls The Widows. This year—Memphis and Nashville, Graceland, the Grand Ole Opry. "Not my first choice," she says, "but I'm open to anywhere without sand."

She asks what his plans are.

"I don't have any, to be honest."

"Are you staying?"

"Yes," he says, although until now, the notion was abstract.

"I was wondering. Winter's different, you know."

"I was here for part of it last year."

"Part's not all. It can be a long stretch." She turns, smiles. "Well, look who it is."

Steven joins them. He wears a thin sweatshirt, shorts that hang to his knees. "Hey Miss Betty."

"How's school going?"

"School's not my favorite." He shrugs off his backpack and sets across the sand.

"He's going to miss you," she says.

Steven wrestles with an umbrella, a battle with the anchoring sand and the breeze-filled canopy. Sometimes Jason

159

CURTIS SMITH

worries about the boy. The origins of their relationship and the feelings Steven might attach to it. Most often, they sit in silence, sharing the shack's shade, but in their conversations, Jason's detected clues. The boy's struggles in school. The father who'll return in the spring, a man who may or may not be in jail.

When Steven brings in the last umbrella, Betty offers a twenty from the shack's cashbox. "You don't need to," Steven says.

"Take it," she says. "I only wish my other employees worked as hard as you."

"Thanks." He slides the bill into his pocket.

Jason locks the shed. "Ms. Betty and I were talking about closing up shop after this weekend."

"It's that time of year," she says.

Steven shields his eyes, and Jason imagines himself from the boy's perspective. The sun in the west, his shadowed face. "When will I see you then?"

Jason loads an armful of folded umbrellas into a trailer. The trailer and pickup his boss's, faded paint and rusted wheel wells. He's already packed and hauled three of Betty's shacks, and he hopes he can finish the rest before dark.

A voice calls, "Hey, Mr. Jason!" Steven runs toward him, waving. An hour earlier, the boy had found him and asked if he could help. Jason told him to ask his mother first, believing she'd say no or the boy would get distracted by his day's next shiny object, but here he is. "My mom says I can hang with you as long as I'm not being a pest and I'm home by supper."

"How come you're not in school?"

"Some kind of teacher day. They work but not us."

"You don't mind working for me then?"

He smiles. "Working for you isn't really work, Mr. Jason. You know what I mean?"

When the trailer is filled, the boy joins Jason in the cab. Jason wrestles the gearshift, his unfamiliarity with stick. The truck lurches from the curb. The windows open, and Steven's voice lifts above the engine's rattle. He talks about school. About his father. About his favorite pro wrestlers and the cool seat he wants to buy for his bike. Steven is nothing like Sophie, yet when Jason talks to the boy, he feels her near. The pauses he takes to find the right words. The desire to offer the truth in the kindest ways possible.

The pickup bucks, and Jason battles the clutch and shifter. "It's hard to think of Ms. Betty driving this thing," Steven says.

"It was her husband's. At least at first. But she can drive it, too."

"Is that Dom?"

"It was." A pause, and he anticipates the boy's next question. "He's been gone a while."

"Oh."

Betty's house is a single-story ranch, a small yard, a two-car garage. Gnomes in a white-stone flowerbed. Her house the kind of simple structure fading beneath the construction of larger dwellings, the summer people, the money that keeps town humming while also crowding out the locals. Jason pulls up the driveway. The garage doors opened, and in the backyard, Betty and the widows—Donna and Linda and Jean, retirees making ends meet on modest pensions and social security, their sunhats and scarves and Crocs. The radio plays, hits from the generation before Jason's. The women spray down and inventory Jason's haul. In the yard's center, the items Betty's selected for disposal—the torn and rusted and bent.

The widows make a fuss over Steven, and in return, the boy works even harder. His huffing earnestness. His slapping flipflops. Betty lays a hand on his shoulder, her face lowered to his ear. "Keep an eye on Jason, OK?"

"Oh, I will."

Jason and Steven return to the truck. Linda calls: "Pick up a six-pack next time!"

"Make it two," Jean says.

"Make sure he doesn't forget, Steven," Donna says.

Steven waves as they back into the street. A smile as Jason grinds his way into drive. "What so funny?" he asks.

Steven shakes his head. "You old people crack me up sometimes."

* * *

J ason sits on the sofa, phone in hand. His mismatched living room. Betty's old rug. A thrift-shop coffee table. A yard-sale couch. The curtains pulled back, this unclaimed morning, and at his feet, a sunlit swatch. The season's last radiant days. He gathers himself then enters the number and the extension.

Arlene is angry at first. She tells him she has nothing to say to him. Tells him he has some nerve, and who does he think he is, calling out of the blue after what he's done. He switches the phone to speaker and sets it on the coffee table. He closes his eyes, imagining her in his kitchen, a wig and shattered glass at their feet. He hears her out, her curses, her venom, and the longer she vents, the more he doubts his decision, the fear he's only capable of offering her more pain. He opens his mouth, a drowning reflex, but no words come. The betrayal of his heart and its half-baked notions. In time, she calms.

"You hurt me."

"I thought I was going to die."

"What did I ever do to you?"

He doesn't speak until she's done, and when he does, he doesn't ask for forgiveness. He tells her he's sorry, tells her he understands his apology means little compared to what he's done. He tells her he's haunted by her face, and if he could go back, he'd put a bullet through his head before ever hurting her again. He tells her his outburst wasn't rooted in that moment, but in the darkness that was eating him alive, and when Arlene asks if she was part of that darkness, he says the scene was, but not her. Never her.

"OK." She sighs. "OK then." A pause. "I'll pray for you."

The words like a fist to his gut, and he gasps. "And I'll pray for you."

They exchange awkward goodbyes. After she hangs up, he stays sitting, elbows on his knees. The pose of a boxer unable to answer the bell. His face in his hands as he sobs.

* * *

J ason wakes from a dream of Alice. A car ride, only neither of them seemed to be driving. A radio he couldn't turn off, the knobs that faded to mist. For a moment, Alice is with him before she's lost to the room's shadows. He sits and swings his feet to the floor. Usually the cat will greet him, rubbing itself against his shins, its hungry mews, but this morning, it's nowhere in sight. He worries it might have slipped out unnoticed, a returning to the wild. He makes kissing noises, his puckered lips. He lowers himself onto hands and knees and discovers the cat beneath his bed. He calls it, coaxing, reassuring, wondering if it senses the day's looming changes.

He puts on a sweatshirt and walks to the corner market. A dark sky. The traffic lights sway on the breeze, and along the curb, the tumble of coffee cups and paper scraps. On the road, pickups with plywood in their beds, and in the opposite direction, the exodus to the bay bridge. The market shelves thinned, and Jason fills his handbasket, cat food, peanut butter and tuna fish, bottled water and bread. A bag of ice. A TV above the checkout, and on it, satellite images of the storm pinwheeling up the coast. Conversations from the others in line. Talk of tides and surges and the mayor's pleas for the infirm and unessential to evacuate.

He walks home, bags in one hand, the ice balanced over his shoulder. Inside, the cat's tail twitches from beneath the bed. Jason turns on the radio. The chatter of meteorologists, the variables at play and the dwindling hopes of being spared. He arranges the food on the countertop. A silent calculation of rations and days. He pauses by the window and thinks of the ocean's power. This thin strip of land. Below, a creeping police van, and Jason opens the window to hear the message from its loudspeaker. The notice that when the storm hits, the bay bridge will close, and all who remain should shelter in place.

Jason sets out on his bike. He watches a man drag his trash-cans into the garage. Another who uses chains and ropes to lash down a backyard trampoline. A gust, and his front wheel wobbles. He passes the church, slowing when he spots the priest and another man filling sandbags. Tufts of the priest's gray hair lift on the breeze. Their shovels dig into the sand that weighs down a pickup's bed.

Jason stops and straddles his bike. "Need a hand, Father?"

The priest straightens, his hands on his back. "If you're able and willing, we'd welcome it."

For the next hour, they fill bags and place them around the church's doors. The other man only speaks Spanish, and the priest, switching languages in mid-sentence, tells stories of past storms, the stained glass he's lost, his hand gesturing the water's height. As Jason shovels, he thinks of a snowstorm last year, the feeling of being a stranger as he stood outside his own home. And he thinks of another snowstorm and the blue palace and the exile of time, a distance greater than any ocean.

When they're done, he shakes hands with the priest and the other man. "Thank you," the priest says. "And take care of yourself."

"Dios sea contigo," the other man says.

Jason pedals to the beach. Gusts funnel between the build-ings. The sway of powerlines. The electricity will give out soon and then the long night. He leaves his bike. The wind stronger atop the dune. The hiss of bent grass, his sweatshirt's rustle. Behind him, workers hurry to secure plywood over ocean-view windows. A few of the curious join him on the beach, and even the big dogs who live to scamper in the surf stand still beside their owners. The churn deafening. An unceasing thunder. The waves fan over the shore's slope and leave tangled seaweed around the lifeguard towers. Above, coils of gray clouds, a sky alive and moving. Sand pelts his sweatshirt, and when the first bands of rain come, the drops angle from the sky and sting his skin. Then the sirens, loud and long. The bay bridge now closed.

Back home, he coaxes the cat from beneath his bed, a respite long enough for it to eat before a window-rattling gust sends it scampering back. Electricity cuts out a few hours later. Jason stands by the window. Rain falls in sheets, the glass blurred. Below, the water already up to the curb, ripples in the wake of the police van, its loudspeaker fighting against the wind and rain and pounding surf as it implores everyone to stay indoors.

The winds pick up, coming and going, the breath of giants. He hangs blankets over the windows, fearful of flying glass, everything dark, his scant belongings captured in a flashlight's passing beam. When the building begins to shake, he slides his mattress partway off the bed, a lean-to fashioned, the floor shared with the cat while the storm rages. A night of sirens and fitful sleep and prayers for this little town along the sea.

The rain eases by dawn. He takes the blankets from the window. The cat leaps onto the ledge, and together, they consider the street's thigh-deep river, the flotsam of plastic and paper, a cooler, a kickball's bright red speck upon the flow. He opens the window, and on the breeze, the smell of the ocean, not the surf but the salt of deep water. A canoe paddles up the street, the man in the back rowing, the one in the front taking pictures. The day passes. Jason eats, looks out the window, sleeps. By nightfall, the water's low enough for the police and fire vehicles to creep past, and in their wakes, ripples that lap the bases of street signs and fire hydrants.

He sleeps again, the day's highjacked rhythms, and when he wakes, it's dark. No streetlights shine upon his window, his room black. His phone out of power, and he feels unclaimed—unclaimed by man, by time and possessions, by purpose. He dresses and heads outside.

The water has receded, but not completely. Moats around sandbags. A gurgling rumble from the sewers, the vibration in his sandaled feet. He walks on, alone, a refugee from an end-of-the-world movie. Soon there will be activity. The city's cleanup crews. The shopkeepers will haul their water-logged goods outside to dry. Insurance adjustors will arrive with their calculators and forms. Doctors and nurses will report for their shifts. The world of useful people while he floats on.

He walks along the outer dune. The gray horizon and thundering sea. The wide beach flattened and wet, and as the sky lightens, shapes rise from the dark. He leaves the dune. His footprints in the wet sand, a path that weaves between the shore's washed-up tangles. Kelp and seaweed. Fish, all dead, their stink in the air, and every so often, a crab, their crooked walks, their blind stagger back to the sea. Cans and bottles and every imaginable vessel of plastic. He walks toward the Point, and the lighthouse's white walls strain from the dark. The debris thicker here, the Point's swirling currents, and soon, he's close enough to see the storm's watermark on the lighthouse's walls, a line well above his head, this stretch lost beneath the merge of ocean and bay, and in the air, the tide's lingering echo.

The debris heavier as he nears the Point. Milk crates. A sign written in a foreign language. Wooden skids. Amid the boulders near the lighthouse's base, an entire tree, its leaves stripped, its weaker branches snapped. A shirt tangled high in its limbs, but as Jason approaches, he realizes the shirt is a man. His head hung, his body twisted. His bare feet dangling high above the sand.

* * *

Betty's teakettle whistles until she removes it from the burner. Sun on her window, autumn's deep blues. The ocean different too, its empty surf, the smell that hangs heavier in the cool air. The kitchen off the dining room, and as she steeps their tea, she tells the story of her girlhood summers here. The house on 11th Street they rented for two weeks every July. The house's screened porch. The shells she collected. The lotion her mother rubbed on her sunburnt shoulders and how she'd cry into her pillow the night before they returned home. On the walls, framed photos. Betty and Dom through the years, youth, old age. Some with her daughter, a woman with her own family now, a new life in a town five hundred miles away.

Betty sets down his cup. "Sure you don't want something stronger?"

He thinks of the bottle he bought Mr. Keane. A walk across a frozen lake. His father. "No, thanks."

She sits. "Have you heard anything about the man you found?"

"No." He blows into the cup, ripples in the dark orange. A week has passed since the storm. Crews are still clearing the beaches and plans are in motion to rebuild the eroded dunes. Three of Betty's shacks were knocked off their foundations, one carried out to sea. "I don't know if they'd tell me even if they did identify him."

"Things like that happen." She sips. "You hear about it, up and down the coast." On the table, a ledger, and from its sides, the bristle of papers and receipts. She slides the ledger toward him. "I appreciate you looking at this."

A few days after he told her he'd worked in finance, Betty asked if he'd help with her books. He'd warned her of his limitations—the difference between studying the market and keeping a clean ledger, his less-than-stellar grades in his two semesters of accounting. He opens the cover.

"Dom's books were immaculate. It was like something an elementary teacher would have kept. Perfect penmanship. Everything checked twice then once again." A tap against his leg, and Betty picks up the black lapdog. The dog half-blind. Its clouded eyes and a snout that twitches in Jason's direction. She kisses the dog between its ears. Jason turns a few pages.

"But as you can see, I'm nothing like Dom. I start out the season OK, but then I forget." Another kiss for the dog's head. "Or more truthfully, I get lazy. I can work all day, but putting numbers in a book after the sun's gone down, I can't bring myself to it. So I just stuff in papers and tell myself I'll get to it later. Which I do, to a lesser or greater extent."

He flips another page. "So what would you like me to do?"

"I just want to be square for tax time. My accountant retired last year. Maybe I drove him to it." She sets the dog down, and it resumes its sniffing of Jason's leg. "And then next year, maybe you can help me start on the good foot. Get some better habits going." She stands. "Let me show you something."

She leaves and returns with another ledger. A sticker on its spine—2015. "Here's how Dom did it." She sits, frowns. "He'd be so disappointed in how I've handled this."

"I think he'd be proud of how you've kept it all going. You said you had a good year."

"We did. At least I think so. But perhaps I've miscalculated. You see the mess I've made."

He opens Dom's ledger. The order of columns and rows, a precision that could have been grafted from Jason's college textbooks. Entries made in pencil then traced over in ink.

"I've kept his old books out and tried to do the same, but I lose focus. I think of him, and I drift, and before I know it, an hour's passed and I've been crying and there's nothing done."

"I understand." He has no idea what follows death—heaven or hell or a landscape beyond his comprehension—yet here is an aspect of death he understands: the empty spaces rendered in the lives left behind, the ghosts carried in the hearts of survivors, and he wonders again about responsibility and what, exactly, the living owe the dead.

"He left me in a good place, money-wise." She sets down a plate of cookies. "He had a life insurance policy. Half a million. We were about to cancel it—it was getting expensive and with our daughter grown and with a new family, we figured we didn't need it anymore. He had the forms signed and the envelope sealed." She breaks a cookie in half and takes a nibble. "And then he died."

"I'm glad he didn't mail it."

"Me too. Put it all in my savings account. Figure it should be more than enough to see me through."

Jason looks up from the ledger. "Wait. You have it all in a savings account?"

Jason pedals home from the supermarket. His wire basket full, more in his backpack. This cold morning. The low sun and his long shadow. The breeze cuts through his jacket. The bike's rusty mechanics. The slip of his tires over the shoulder's sand. He thinks about the ocean, this melting world, and the water that will erase, not in a flood but a creeping inch at a time, this town and a thousand like it.

He turns into an alley. A passage narrow and shadowed. He catches sight of the boy—a moment's recognition before Steven ducks behind a dumpster. Jason stops, straddles his bike. "Steven?"

The boy steps from behind the dumpster. He looks down at his sneakers. "Hey, Mr. Jason."

"Why're you hiding?"

"No reason." Seagulls overhead, and the cries echo along the alley's brick.

"It's a school day, isn't it?"

The boy nudges a stone with his sneaker. "Probably."

"Probably?"

"Yeah." He shrugs. "Yeah, I guess."

Jason gets off his bike. "You're not going to hide out here all day." He nods toward the dumpster. "It's kind of stinky."

A reluctant grin. "Yeah."

"Want to come with me? I'm going to go check on the shack after I drop this off."

"Check what?"

"Just to make sure everything's OK. The storm and everything. Some of them got damaged, you know."

A quick stop at Jason's apartment. His supermarket take

unloaded, and before he locks the door, a glance from the living room window. The boy below, standing guard over a worthless bike. How small he looks.

Jason walks his bike on the way to the beach. The boy beside him. Their shadows on the sidewalk. The boy quiet. Stones kicked along the gutter. The breeze picks up as they cross the oceanfront road, then stronger again as they crest the outer dunes. More gulls, wings spread, motionless above the surf. A balance struck between water and sky.

Steven circles the shed, inspecting from top to bottom. "It looks OK."

"We lost a few."

"The storm was crazy. We had off school for the rest of the week. That was nice." He studies the waves. "I heard they found a guy washed up by the lighthouse."

"I heard that, too." Jason wonders what the boy recalls from beneath the water. Wonders if, in his stillest moments, he remembers the surf's thunder or his body's ragdoll dance or what it was like to stand before the dead.

They cross the road. An exchange—Jason carrying the backpack, Steven on the bike, a wobbling path. He gets off after a block and walks the bike. The boy's steps slower as they near the school. "I know I need to go," he says.

Jason thinks of all he's left behind. "It's hard. Facing things. I know."

"I'm already pretty late. If the principal is around, she's going to be mad."

"Late's better than absent."

At the entrance steps, they exchange the bike for the backpack. "How's Betty doing?" Steven asks.

"Good. I'll tell her you were asking about her."

Halfway up the stairs, he pauses. The sun upon him, and

he shields his eyes. "You think she'll let me work with her this summer maybe? Maybe with you?"

"I think we should ask her."

Steven waits at the entrance. A button pushed. A buzz and an opened door, and he's gone without looking back.

* * *

The view from the bay bridge's hump, a final glimpse of sun-touched water, then inland, his car picking up speed, and the ocean's scent fades into pine. Other smells—the black coffee he sips, the passenger seat's lilies. He hasn't driven this far since the night he left, a route he now retraces. A homecoming to a place that's no longer home.

Hours slip by, the sun higher as he passes beneath the cemetery arch. The winding lane, and around him, fields of stones. He's early, and part of him worries about finding his way—the haze of memory, the landscape's repetition—but this isn't the case. He parks, gets out. A breeze, and he zips his jacket. An oak's branches clatter, hollow notes, and he stands, waiting, flowers in hand.

She pulls up a few minutes later. She wears sunglasses and a long, black coat. In her gloved hands, a pair of lilies and the weakest of smiles when she notices his. They've talked a couple times since finalizing the divorce. Practical matters mostly, but he reached out about today a few weeks ago, a hoping not for reconciliation but for a moment's grace. She takes off her sunglasses, and he wants to embrace her, the urge an ambush, the realization he hasn't held someone close since the afternoon he pulled a half-drowned boy from the surf.

"Hey," he says.

"Hey."

"Thank you." The flowers' plastic sleeve crinkles. "Thank you for coming."

She nods. "Ready?"

They walk together. A squirrel bounds ahead of them. Finches peck the grass. Here is their New Year's, their anniversary, the alpha and omega of their calendar days. He feels the years' rush—the dwindling before and the ever-growing after. Yet despite his wounded heart, there is a lightness this cold morning. The feeling of stepping outside himself. A stripping of masks and shells.

They pause at her stone. Alice crouches, her ritual, a picking of grass, a kiss of her fingers and her hand laid upon the carved name. He wonders if she's come here in his absence, and he decides she has. When she stands, he takes her place. His hand upon the stone. Before, he'd felt Sophie below, trapped, alone, but his feelings have changed. In the ground, the body that betrayed her—but when he walks the beach, he sometimes feels her close. Not the singular her he knew and loved but something more expansive and harder to define, a migration from the physical into a hundred mysterious tides. And when he thinks this way, he considers the strangers who've gathered at the ocean's edge, and in their faces, the same mysteries, all of them counting down their finite breaths. All of them toeing the edge of the greater sea.

He lays his lily beside hers, and when he stands, a dizzy rush, this morning without eating, his knotted stomach and too much coffee. They each hold a lily, and he offers her his. Alice smiles and does the same, and after the exchange, she tucks her hair behind her ear. "It's good to think about her. It hurts, but it's good."

"She couldn't have asked for a better mother."

Alice sucks her lip. "I see her sometimes, around the house. I talk to her."

"She's still with us. In some ways. When I need her most."

"It pains me, her knowing what we've done. Who we've become."

"I know." He wants to say more, his belief that if there is a next life, she'd understand, that she'd see their frailties the way he once looked upon her as a child—a creature innocent in her unknowing—but such words are beyond him, and all he can offer is an echo: "I know."

They stand in silence, their shadows across her stone. "I don't have the poem." He reaches into his pocket and retrieves his phone. "I could pull it up—"

Alice closes her eyes, a pause before she speaks:

"When, in disgrace with fortune and men's eyes,
I all alone beweep my outcast state,
And trouble deaf heaven with my bootless cries,
And look upon myself and curse my fate,
Wishing me like to one more rich in hope,
Featured like him, like him with friends possessed,
Desiring this man's art and that man's scope,
With what I most enjoy contented least;
Yet in these thoughts myself almost despising,
Haply I think on thee, and then my state,

She hesitates. The wind in the trees and the cold sun upon them. He picks up, surprising himself, the words flooding back, and she joins him by the line's end.

Like to the lark at break of day arising
From sullen earth sings hymns at heaven's gate:
For thy sweet love remembered such wealth brings
That then I scorn to change my state with kings."

She sighs. "I need to get back to work."

On the walk to their cars, a misstep, her low heels, the grass's dips. He reaches out, her hand in his until they reach the cemetery lane.

* * *

The wind funnels through town's cross streets. Above, the sway of weathered Christmas decorations, candy canes, stars and angels and bells. Tomorrow is Christmas Eve, and in the windows of stores and apartments, the glow of lights. The supermarket checkout girls in floppy Santa hats. A car beeps, and even though Jason doesn't see who's driving, he waves, and the act makes him feel a little less lonely. Just the locals now, the born-and-bred. Then the ones like him, the ones carried upon random tides, and among them, another division. The ones who take root and the others destined to disappear with the next storm.

The bookstore. Last-minute shoppers and Christmas carols on the speakers. An old man at the magazine stand. In the children's section, a woman with an infant on her knee, another page turned in a board book. The child's fingers buried in its cooing mouth. Jason thinks of Sophie's overflowing shelves, all the things he wanted her to know. He picks up a sketchbook, new pencils, a gift for himself. In the next aisle, a book about the ocean. He opens the book, and the pages fan. Pictures upon pictures—whales and sharks, the bright wonders of the coral reef. A smile as he studies the illustrated relationship between moon and tide. At the register, a woman with reindeer antlers asks if he'd like his things wrapped.

"Just the book, please."

Outside, and he cinches his collar against the wind. The alcove beside the drugstore smells of spilled beer. Its walls of peeling paint, fliers for yard sales and lost dogs. He reads the mailboxes' names and presses a button. A voice sputters over the intercom, and Jason holds his face close to the speaker. A buzz, and he opens the door.

The stairwell narrow and steep, the hitch in his knee, and he's thankful their apartment is on the second floor and not the fourth. 2B's door opens, and there's Steven, his Eagles sweatshirt, a towel around his shoulders, and for Jason, a memory, the summer Sophie fell in love with superheroes. The homemade cape she wore everywhere she went.

"Hey, Mr. Jason." The boy beams, a different kind of light in this dim hallway. "My mom is just about to cut my hair."

His mother behind him. Her dark hair let down, its tips brushing her shoulders. Her work uniform exchanged for a sweater. From behind the hallway's closed doors, hints of other lives. Scents from simmering pots, muffled voices. In her hand, scissors and a comb.

"Sorry if I'm interrupting."

She smiles. "I'm sure Steven is happy for the reprieve."

"I don't like getting my hair cut."

"It's more like he's not a fan of sitting still." She steps back, the door opened wider. "Would you like to come in?"

"No, thank you." He reaches into his bag and hands the wrapped book to Steven. "Santa asked me to drop this off."

The boy shakes his head. "There's no Santa, Mr. Jason. You know that." He turns the book over in his hands. "Can I open it?"

His mother rests a hand on his head. Behind her, a tiny Christmas tree, ornaments of red and blue. "Don't you mean 'thank you'?"

"Thank you. Can I open it?"

"I'll let you and your mom work that out after you get your haircut."

"That's very kind," she says. For a moment, he mistakes the tenderness in her eyes for desire, but no. Hers is the gaze of one lonely heart recognizing another.

"I've intruded enough." He steps back. "You two have a good Christmas."

The boy lingers in the doorway. The towel around his shoulders. "You too, Mr. Jason. Merry Christmas."

* * *

He wakes to snow falling outside his window. The white like static. The familiar blurred. He makes coffee and pulls a chair to the window. Steam from his mug, and in the street, cars made identical beneath the white. The stillness interrupted by a passing pickup. The spin of its back tires, tracks in the snow.

The cat arches against his legs as he puts on his boots. Outside, and he breathes in the hush. There are stretches where his are the snow's first footprints, and he thinks of the summer that's passed and the one to come, and despite the chill, neither feels distant, this life of cycles and seasons and tides. The only finite trajectory the one he's shackled to, an arrow shot into the sky, rising then stalling and then . . .

He crosses the ocean-front road and struggles to the top of the outer dune. A slip of his boots, this odd footing. He's witnessed hundreds of snowfalls, but here's a new sight. A beach frosted in white. A moonscape untouched, and beyond, the march of a million flakes into the waves.

* * *

Winter's early evening. On his dining room table, sorted piles. Receipts and invoices. Permits. Pay stubs. At the table's center, Betty's open ledger. All of it a mess. A puzzle missing half its pieces. He's sat down with her a few times. Their plans to keep better records next year—more so, his suggestions for investments. Explanations and options. Treasury bills and CDs and fixed annuities. The college fund she's set up for her granddaughter. His phone buzzes as he turns the ledger's next page.

Talk?

His pecking finger. *Of course.*

A ring, and he gathers himself before speaking. "Hey."

"Hey," she says.

"All OK?"

"No. Hold on." In the background, voices, an intercom. An elevator's ding. Sounds from his dreams. "Are you at the hospital?"

"It's my dad."

"Is he OK?"

"He had a heart attack. He was gone for a minute or two, but they brought him back."

"Jesus. I'm sorry." He stands at the window. The darkness. The ocean beyond.

"It was his community's pickleball tournament. The championship game. You know how he gets. But he's resting now. He's hooked up to a half dozen machines." Her voice lowers. "The first thing he did when he opened his eyes was pull back his oxygen mask and . . ."

She says nothing, and after a moment, he asks, "Alice?"

"He said he saw Sophie." She sighs. "He said she was full

182

of light. Radiant. He said he touched her hand and felt the light in him before he was pulled back."

Jason lays a hand on the window glass. He feels the cold, the surf and wind. "Our Sophie."

"Our Sophie."

Neither speaks, a silence both solitary and shared. Jason breaks the spell. "And your mom? How's she?"

"Frightened. Relieved. Shocked."

"Do you need anything? I can leave right now." The words a reflex. The desire to place his hands alongside hers and cup their child's glow. To remember her as the rest of the world forgets.

"No, that's OK. But thanks." Then quieter, "I just wanted you to know."

He can't tell if she means her father's heart attack or his vision. "I appreciate it." He sits on the floor and pets the cat. "Give them my best. If you think that's a good move."

"I should go back." A pause. "I wasn't interrupting anything, was I?"

"No, not at all. And call if you need anything or if anything changes."

"I will. I just needed to hear your voice."

She hangs up, and he holds his phone, studying a picture of their girl until the screen goes dark.

Betty makes lunch, humming along with the oldies station on the kitchen radio. Jason checks out her living room's shelves. There's a framed photo of the widows posed before Graceland's gates. A piece of driftwood, the holes that give it the appearance of a flute. He picks up a plastic viewer, a trinket no larger than his thumb, and holds it to his eye. Inside, a photo of Betty and Dom and their infant daughter. A sandcastle and a beautiful sky, Dom and the girl holding plastic shovels. The colors faded. He aims the viewer toward the window, the figures, for a moment, infused with sunshine.

Betty sets down their sandwiches, but before they eat, they go over his paperwork. She signs where he tells her—here, here, here—not paying attention to his explanations, the pen handed back with a sigh when they're done.

"This year will be different," Jason says. "We'll have a system for keeping records. We'll stay on top of our entries. It'll make things easier."

"I don't know. I get tired just thinking about it." She takes a small bite and returns her sandwich to the tray. "Most places have their rentals in shops in town. Not Dom. 'Keep them where the people are,' he said." She smiles. "Me, I know better. He just wanted to be with those folks on the beach, not behind a counter." Her finger taps the table. "What about you?"

"What about me?"

"I've been thinking about selling."

"Selling to me?"

"Selling in general, but asking you first. You seem to like the scene." She nods to the ledger and papers. "You're good with this side of things."

His first inclination is a flat no, but he hesitates. He thinks about what the business meant to Dom—and in turn, what Dom meant to her—and he thinks about Sophie and the magic that lingers in the things she'd touched and loved.

She speaks before he can answer. "Think about it."

A knock, and when she answers the door, the widows file in. The cold carried on their shed knit caps and winter coats. The widows each carry a folder or shoebox, and as they settle around the table and turn their smiling faces upon him, Jason feels like he's missed out on some inside joke.

Betty goes to the kitchen and fills the kettle. "I told the ladies about the help you gave me with my portfolio. And they were wondering if you could give them some pointers, too."

Jason wrestles the gearshift as the pickup chugs over the bay bridge. The windows cracked, his fear of fumes, the floorboards' rot. The cab's seashell hum and the bay's salty breeze. The empty trailer bucks. Betty beside him, giving directions, the whip of her hair. The flatland's pines reflected in her sunglasses.

They pass houses, woodsmoke from their chimneys. Boats and trailers parked on sandy drives. Rusted cars half buried in weeds. Betty thanks Jason for driving. This yearly ritual, a trip she's made alone since Dom's death, and between her and Jason, an unspoken kinship—the hauntings of who they've loved and who they've lost—the details less important than the lenses that color their days.

The distributor waits an hour inland. A lot surrounded by a chain-link fence, a cinder-block main building and a storage garage large enough to hold three trucks. An old dog sleeps atop the office stairs, its head lifted as they park, Betty pausing to stroke its head before she goes inside. She emerges with a white-haired man. A gimpy stride, a boot that whispers across the gravel. Betty's steps slowed to stay by his side, the dog trotting behind. The old man's coat with its oil-stained cuffs. A cigarette brought to his mouth, an exhale and a smile of yellowed teeth.

Betty introduces Mike. The men shake, Mike's palms callused, the dirt beneath his nails. Mike takes a final drag and grinds his cigarette butt beneath his boot. The dog lies down, his head between its outstretched paws, its eyes upon its master. Mike and Betty catch up. Easy to understand the history between them. The years and the struggles. The growing list of those no longer around. The bond of survival.

Mike enters the garage's shadows and returns with a chair and an umbrella. He unfolds the chair, opens the umbrella. On each, a logo of yellow and blue, the colors of sun and sky, and at the center, **DOM'S RENTALS**. Betty drapes an arm over Mike's shoulders. "Perfect."

On the way home, the umbrellas and chairs rattle in the trailer. The sun bright, an illumination of the windshield's dirt, the morning's chill eased. Jason raises his voice above the engine's clatter. He thanks her for the offer to sell but proposes another plan. A year where she'll step back but still be in charge. A division of duties. A season to learn from one another. A handshake as they're lifted by the bay bridge. Beneath them, the sun upon the water. Fishermen setting out to sea.

* * *

Dee answers the door. A pointy cardboard hat atop her head. A polite scolding when Jason hands her a wrapped gift. "Told you not to."

He steps inside, and she shuts the door. "It's nothing big." He thinks of the harmonica beneath the paper. "Perhaps you'll end up wishing I hadn't brought it at all."

The apartment not so different than his. The open floor of living and dining rooms, a kitchen, a poor man's lines of sight. A box fan in the window, the ocean's scent, and the breeze lifts the letters of a sagging banner—*Happy Birthday*. Steven and a few other boys gathered in front of the TV. All in cardboard hats. Steven and another boy work video game controllers, their intent gazes and busy hands, and on the screen, cars race through city streets. One of the cars crashes, and with the spell broken, Steven looks Jason's way. "Hey, Mr. Jason. There's cake if you want some."

On the table, a sheet cake, the boy's birthday greeting lopped off in little squares. Dee hands Jason a plate and a plastic fork. She introduces another woman, the mother of the boy who feared his best friend had drowned. The woman's face lights, a lingering handshake. "So this is our hero." The man sitting near the fan stands when Dee steers Jason his way. "And this," she says, "is Oscar, Steven's father."

Oscar sets down his plate with its half-eaten slice of cake and wipes his palm against his jeans before offering it. The chase on the TV continues. The boys' trash talk. The squeal of tires. Oscar's shorter than Jason. A barbwire tattoo around his bicep. His black hair shaved close and tight. His grip strong. "I've got a lot to thank you for."

188

"Right place, right time," Jason says. "I'm just glad I was there."

"No, I mean it." Shouts from the living room, and on the screen, a fiery wreck. "We all owe you."

Dee places a hat on Jason's head, and when he secures the elastic strap, he thinks of a mask he wore on a cold night. A mansion in the country, a room lit in red and blue. The twisting of nameless flesh. Steven brings his empty cup, and his father fills it, the table's array of soda, a pat on the head before the boy returns to his friends. Oscar sits, and as Jason eats his cake, he aligns Oscar with the fragments Dee and Steven have shared. A high school romance. An army stint. Pregnancy and marriage. Another tour, but when he returned, the troubles started. He wasn't angry so much as raw. Sleep difficult. The nights he wandered the streets and the good job he lost. He fell in with his old high school crowd. Troublemakers. Petty thieves. Then the drunken night he stole a truck and punched a cop, his fifteen-month absence explained to Steven as another tour. He and Dee neither divorced nor together. "You know the saying 'it's complicated'?" she explained the evening she stopped by to invite Jason to the party. "Well, this isn't—either he gets his shit together or we're done."

The evening ebbs into night, and with the dark, Dee turns off the fan. The boys play a new game, this one with guns, men hunting each other through a bombed-out city, a glance from Dee to Oscar, who turns off the screen with a click of the remote, the boys complaining until he proposes they head up to the roof to set off the fireworks he's brought.

Dee frets on their single-file ascent. The noise, the complaints of neighbors. Her voice echoes in the stairwell, admonishments for the boys to be careful, to stay away from the roof's edge. Two floors then a door marked **Keep out**. The last stairwell narrow, the space warm and unlit. Oscar in the lead, a fiddling with the deadbolts before the door atop the stairs swings back. The push of cooler air, the boys' excited voices, and when Jason steps onto the flat tarpaper, the sky opens. The stars above the streetlights, and to the east, just beyond the town's lights, the surf's white curl. Dee calls after the boys who chase one another—no running, stay away from the parapet. Steven sets down his box, and the boys gather round. Oscar supervises, both warning and encouraging. Sparklers held in waving hands. Roman candles. Rockets nestled in empty beer bottles. Fuses lit, colored explosions reflected in the boys' heaven-turned eyes. Oscar sneaks a flask from his jacket pocket and tips it into his plastic cup. He stands next to Jason as rockets hiss into the dark.

"Thanks again," Oscar says. "I keep imagining him not here. I don't know if I could handle that."

Another explosion, then the next. Blue. White. "He's a good kid."

Oscar sips, an inhale between pursed lips. "Don't know what you know. About Dee and me."

"Nothing specific."

"I'm trying to keep it together. Trying to walk the right path. It's hard sometimes, forgiving. Not her—me. It's hard forgiving yourself. I don't even know if it's possible."

"I know what you mean. I'm hoping it's possible." Another explosion, a bloom of sparks. "Forgetting might not be in the cards, but perhaps that's a good thing."

The boys arrange their grand finale. A dozen rockets fly. Steven and the other boys salute. Oscar sticks his fingers in the corners of his mouth and lets out a shrill whistle. Then the silence. The gunpowder residue scatters on the breeze.

Jason offers his goodbyes outside the apartment door. The boys rush past to reboot their game. Dee thanks him again, a handshake from Oscar. Jason's apartment only a block away, yet he opts for a stroll along the ocean-front road. Quiet houses on one side, the sea's dark on the other. He thinks about loneliness and the comfort of shadows. Thinks of the moat he's dug around his heart and the fear not of being hurt but of hurting another.

He's washing the day's dishes when his buzzer rings. The sound catches him off guard, this year without visitors. Steven's voice on the intercom, and after buzzing them in, he opens the door to discover the boy bounding up the steps, his mother behind. Steven holds up a plastic bag. "We got some ice cream to go with the last of the cake. Rocky Road."

"Are we interrupting?" Dee asks. An expression very different than her son's.

"Please, come in." Jason steps aside. The boy flops onto the couch. He reaches for the cat, who leaps away and hides beneath a chair.

"My dad would have come but he's locked himself on the roof." Steven pulls the harmonica from his sweatshirt's pouch. "We're waiting on the super."

"Can I put this in the freezer?" Dee asks.

She follows Jason to the kitchen, a view of the living room, the back of Steven's head. "Hey, don't you have a TV?"

"Sorry."

"Hmm." He toots sour notes on the harmonica. He pauses. "Hey, thanks for this, Mr. Jason. It's pretty cool." He goes back to playing.

They linger in the cramped kitchen, and Dee whispers. "I'm sorry. I didn't know where else to bring him." Her eyes wet. The boy blows a high note then a low. "He's on the roof, but he's not locked out. He's not in a good place. He's been drinking." She rubs her face. "I just didn't want Steven around if there was a scene. I didn't—"

"Did you call anyone?"

"His brother, but I had to leave a message. I'm afraid to call the police. Afraid of what that could trigger." She rubs her eyes, and her lips tremble. "I don't know. I just don't know."

He gets two bowls from a cabinet. "Give me the key and let me go over. At least until his brother gets in touch." He scoops ice cream into the bowls. From the living room, the harmonica's screech.

She offers her keys, and her hand lingers in his. "He's not a bad person. He really isn't."

She sets the bowls on the coffee table. Jason tells Steven he has to go to the store before it closes, the promise to be right back, and when he returns, they'll pull up some videos about playing the harmonica. He pauses at the door. Mother and son consider him from the couch, each with their different understandings of the night, the stories waiting in their eyes.

Jason approaches the drug store. His gaze lifts. The street's valley of light, the dark sky, and he imagines Oscar alone, suspended between the two. Jason lets himself in. He checks the apartment first. A still life. A moment interrupted—the dishes and cake, the torn wrappers, an empty harmonica box. He closes the door and goes to the top floor. A pause at the unbolted door before he steps out.

The sea air, the wide sky, and he breathes easier. The tarpaper littered with spent fireworks and plastic cups. He's about to go back in when he spots the shadowed form sitting against the alley-side parapet.

"Hey," Jason says.

Oscar raises his flask. Captured light in the glass, a glimmer in the dark. "Here comes the cavalry, saving the day again."

"Mind if I sit?"

"Help yourself."

Jason rests his back against the parapet. The day's warmth

in the tarpaper, the evening's chill on his face. Oscar offers the flask. "No, thanks," Jason says.

Oscar shrugs. "What did she say?"

"She's concerned."

Waves pound along the shore. The two men silent, this communion, their lives so different yet the most important elements shared. The wreckage of their pasts. Their hazy futures. Oscar takes a sip then lowers the flask. "I should have been the one to save him. I should have been there when he needed me."

"He needs you now." Jason looks up. The stars, this dark, this drowning. He fills his lungs. "I lost my daughter. Sophie." The word heavy, the months it's been locked inside him. "She was sick, and all the prayers and all the money in the world couldn't save her." He rubs his face. "Then I lost more. Everything. And I couldn't have done anything to save my girl, but all the rest was on me."

A pause, "I'm sorry, man."

"I did a lot of shit I wish I could forget, but I don't think forgetting is in the cards for me." He's back upon the ice. The cold. The crack beneath his feet. The birds in the naked trees. "And I tried to throw it all away because living felt no different than dying."

Oscar's finger taps the flask's side. "Yeah."

"So I'm here, trying to figure it all out, but I guess I'll never do that. But the trying let me be here that day for Steven. And for that, I'm grateful."

"Maybe God put you there."

Jason pictures the stained glass in St. Brendan's, two men upon a raging sea. "I don't think everything happens for a reason, but maybe sometimes reason finds us. Maybe we just have to be there, ready. Our eyes and hearts open."

Oscar nods. They sit, not talking until Jason asks, "Think you're ready to go in?"

Oscar stands, stretches. "Yeah." A wobble with his first steps. Jason opens the stairwell door. "Want a ride?"

"I think a walk would be good for my head."

On the sidewalk, they shake hands and go their separate ways. At the corner, Jason looks back. Oscar beneath a street-light, a silhouette, then a fade into the night.

* * *

He wakes hours before dawn. A dream that feels vital, images that slip between his fingers. He dresses. The cat lifts its head, blinks, and goes back to sleep.

He walks to the beach. The streets still, the dark windows, and he remembers the frigid night he stood outside Nathan's townhouse. That world of dreamers and the evil in his soul. He's thankful not to be that man anymore, yet he can't say what kind of man he is. Sometimes he believes he's nothing. He's air; he's water. He's a sketchbook's blank page. He sits atop the outer dune. The wind's chill and the warmth beneath his sweatshirt. The surf as steady as his pulse. The eastern sky begins its bleed, and he thinks of the sunrises he's witnessed. Each a snapshot. Each a footprint in the sand.

The sun inches above the horizon, a path burnt across the water, and he squints. He thinks of the universe's cold reach and the miracle of warmth upon his face. He stands, wipes off his pants. His joints stiff. In town, the sun lifts the rooftop of Steven's building from the shadows, and along the street below, the day's first stirrings. Delivery trucks. Shop owners unlocking their doors. A gray man walking a gray dog says, "Good morning." A diner, and from its kitchen, the scent of bread. In Jason's pocket, a folded ten, and he goes in.

The booths empty, only one other customer at the counter, a turned back. The waitress young, a tired smile. "Thank you," Jason says when she brings his coffee and English muffin. The morning paper on the counter. A gunman on the loose. An earthquake on the other side of the world. Music from the kitchen radio. The door's chime rings, and a young man holding an infant enters. The waitress steps from behind the counter, an embrace for the man, and a kiss for the baby's fore-head. Wishes for a good day and the promise to see each other soon. The man holds the infant's wrist, a wave for the mother. Jason's back to them, the scene witnessed in the mirror behind the counter, and when they exit, he's left alone with his reflection. He finishes his coffee and places the ten on the counter.

He walks through town, lifted by the coffee, by the stirring life on the streets and sidewalks, yet also feeling the pull to return to bed. The sun higher, and with its light, a memory of summer. Soon the crowded markets and sidewalk bustle, the night voices rising to his opened window. He walks on, and as he nears St. Brendan's, he sees the priest, only today, his left arm is in a cast. The priest struggles, the broom's weak sway. The broom strikes the entrance's handrail and clatters down the steps.

Jason crosses the street, and when the priest drops the broom again, Jason picks it up. "Let me," he says.

"Thank you." A pause, a searching for recognition. "You're the man who helped with the sandbags. Before the storm."

"Yes."

"You have a knack for coming by at the right time."

"I'm glad that's the case." He sweeps the entranceway, the steps.

"There's a funeral in a few hours. It's nice to have things in order for the family." The fingers sticking out of his cast flex. "This accident has made some things challenging."

Jason reaches the walkway, the priest beside him as he sweeps. "Is the other man who helped with the sandbags around?"

The priest shakes his head. "He's in jail, I'm afraid."

"Sorry to hear that."

"I pray for him. We're all in the dark, even sometimes the ones who've seen the light."

Jason nods. The broom whispers against the pavement. When they reach the sidewalk's end, Jason hands back the broom. "Take care, Father."

* * *

E vening, the Tuesday before Memorial Day. A warm afternoon, a sky of pale clouds. Betty and the widows at a spa retreat, massages and mud baths, a final respite before the season. Steven's school year in its lazy winddown. Jason's day spent in Betty's pickup, the trailer weighed with the umbrellas and chairs and boogie boards he delivered to Dom's shacks. The trailer unhitched and left back in Betty's driveway. The pickup's windows down, and in the cab, the whip of wind, a seashell's hum as he drives the lonely road to the Point.

The road dead-ends into an empty gravel lot. They park and make their way across the sand. The sun over the bay, this golden hour. The lighthouse rises from the Point's rocks, its halo of circling gulls, and he thinks of a storm's wake, the beach and its wreckage. A dead man in a tree.

He can't erase what he's done, and he can't erase what he's suffered. He's run until he could run no further, and still the world found him and flowed over him—death, survival, sadness, uncertainty—and what choice does he have beyond surrendering to or embracing the tide?

The surf calm today, but he knows appearances at the Point can be deceiving. They kick off their sandals, lay their shirts over their towels. Their shadows stretch before them as they near the water. The surf pushes up, froth around their ankles. A shudder in Alice's shoulders. "It's cold," she says.

She pulls the wind-blown hair from her face and tucks it behind her ear. She's accepted his invitation to come down for a few days, another testing of the waters. He thinks of the book he gave Steven, an illustration of the ocean's layers, its zones of light and life. The backwash pulls at his ankles. His toes lost beneath the sand.

Another step, and they gasp as a wave rolls over them. "Yes," she says when he asks if she's up for this.

They step out again, and then a wave so cold it steals his breath, and before the next one, they dive and emerge with a gasp beyond the breakers. The water lifts and lowers them, nudging them toward the shore then nudging them back. Unseen, the rhythm of their arms, the bicycling of their legs. This dance to keep their heads above water. His lips tremble, and he knows their time here is short. He reaches out, and beneath the surface, they hold hands, riding out a swell and then the one after that and the one after that and the one

ACKNOWLEDGMENTS

Thanks as always to Lisa Kastner, Peter Wright, Evangeline Estropia, and the rest of the Running Wild team for helping bring this book into the world.

And the deepest of thanks to my family for their patience, understanding, and support as I continue this journey.

ACKNOWLEDGMENTS

ABOUT RUNNING WILD PRESS

Running Wild Press publishes stories that cross genres with great stories and writing. RIZE publishes great genre stories written by people of color and by authors who identify with other marginalized groups. Our team consists of:

Lisa Diane Kastner, Founder and Executive Editor
Cody Sisco, Acquisitions Editor, RIZE
Benjamin White, Acquisition Editor, Running Wild
Peter A. Wright, Acquisition Editor, Running Wild
Resa Alboher, Editor
Angela Andrews, Editor
Sandra Bush, Editor
Ashley Crantas, Editor
Rebecca Dimyan, Editor
Abigail Efird, Editor
Aimee Hardy, Editor
Henry L. Herz, Editor
Cecilia Kennedy, Editor
Barbara Lockwood, Editor

Scott Schultz, Editor
Rod Gilley, Editor

Evangeline Estropia, Product Manager
Kimberly Ligutan, Product Manager
Lara Macaione, Marketing Director
Joelle Mitchell, Licensing and Strategy Lead
Pulp Art Studios, Cover Design
Standout Books, Interior Design
Polgarus Studios, Interior Design

Learn more about us and our stories at www.runningwild-press.com

Loved these stories and want more? Follow us at runningwildpublishing.com, www.facebook.com/runningwild-press, on Twitter @lisadkastner @RunWildBooks

RUNNING WILD
RUNNING WILD PRESS

www.ingramcontent.com/pod-product-compliance
Lightning Source LLC
Chambersburg PA
CBHW051134020726
47501CB00005B/1497